DOPPEL

BANG ENOUGH FROGS AND ONE'S BOUND TO BECOME A PRINCE...*RIGHT???*

BANGER

A ROMANTIC COMEDY
HEATHER M. ORGERON

ALSO BY HEATHER M. ORGERON

Vivienne's Guilt
Boomeranger
Breakaway
Doppelbanger

For Ashley—

My world is a darker place without you in it.

DOPPEL

BANG ENOUGH FROGS AND ONE'S BOUND TO BECOME A PRINCE...*RIGHT???*

BANGER

Chapter One

GINA

I love men. *Young* men. Ones who aren't looking for anything more than a good time. Cuz I am nothing if not a good time. I'm what a lot of people in this hole-in-the-wall town refer to as a *cougar*. Well, let the busybodies talk. I'm not fucking anyone's husband or daddy. I like 'em completely unattached—preferably with a nice-sized dick and just enough experience to know how to use it.

It's not that I have anything against guys my own age, or even older men. It's just that I'm not looking to settle down. *Ever*. And at thirty-five, there aren't many guys my age who are still single and aren't looking to plant their asses in one spot and put down some roots. You can think of me more like moss—mobile.

I don't have commitment issues, and I've got nothing against children. I just can't have them. That kind of puts a damper on the whole roots situation. The last thing I need is some guy fancying himself in love with me and giving up his dream of a family, then resenting me the rest of our miserable existence. Ain't nobody got time for that.

This isn't my sob story, and I don't want anyone feeling sorry for me. I won't go as far as to say I'm okay with it, but it is what it is, and I've accepted it. Might as well make the most of my situation and have a little fun while I'm at it. Am I right?

To settle my biological clock, which to my dismay did not break along with my useless female organs, I'm super close to my godsons. My best friend Spencer and I raised them together until she married her high school sweetheart, Cooper, two years ago. At this very moment, they're adding two little girls to our brood. And I'm on my way to the hospital with her fifteen-year-old twins, Lake and Landon, and their four-year-old son, Kyle, a.k.a. Savage, to meet their new sisters.

"Auntie Gigi?" a curious little voice calls from the back seat.

"Yes, Kyle?"

"How did my sisters get inside Mommy's tummy?" *Oh, shit.* No matter how I answer this, I know I'm going to wind up getting myself into trouble. A cold sweat breaks out across my forehead, and my heart rate kicks up a notch.

Just when I'm about to hammer the nail into my own coffin, Landon jumps in, saving me from myself. "Your daddy put these little seeds, called sperms, inside of the eggs in Mommy's tummy, and the babies grew."

Sighing with relief, I glance over to the passenger seat at my teenaged hero. "Thanks, Landon."

"No problem, Aunt Gina." He shakes his head, his lips curling into a little smirk.

"Is that how I gotted in Mommy's tummy too?" Savage asks his brother, who in turn clears his throat loudly.

"Well, no...Because, you know how Cooper adopted you?"

I watch as Kyle's head nods through the rearview mirror.

"Well, a man named Alex put his sperm in Mommy's egg, and you grew in her tummy."

Realization dawns on his little face. "And let me guess... that asshole Tate putted his sperms in her eggs to grow y'all?"

The boys burst into hysterics as I bite down on my lips, fighting to contain my own laughter. I should probably make it known right away that there is a damn good reason we all refer to Kyle as a savage.

"Well..." A choked laugh escapes my pursed lips as I maneuver my little Audi into a spot in the hospital parking garage. "I don't think any of us will argue with you on that logic."

This line of questioning continues as we navigate the halls, trying to find our way to labor and delivery. It's all very sweet and innocent until he drops the atomic bomb. "But, Auntie, how did *all* those men get their seeds in my mom's tummy?"

My throat dries up, and I've suddenly lost the ability to move my feet. My hand lifts to scrub over my face.

"Yeah, Gigi," Lake encourages, clearly delighted by this question. "How did *allll* those men get their sperm in there?"

My eyes narrow to little slits. "You are dead to me," I growl.

Lake and Landon flank my sides, their arms crossed on their newly muscled chests, awaiting my downfall. I can feel their beady blue eyes burning holes through my cheeks. "Well, umm. You see...the sperm are stored in little uh...compartments called testicles, and when a man wants to make a baby with a woman—usually his wife...he can shoot them into her vagina with his penis...like a water gun."

Spit flies from their evil teenaged mouths as they fold over, laughing. *Fuckers.* "Don't either of you ever ask me for another thing, ever again. I swear to God," I hiss, realizing we've stopped right in front of Spencer's room. I shoulder past the still-smirking boys and push the door open before Kyle can ask any more questions.

My EYES WELL UP WHEN we step inside. Spencer's mom, Mrs. Elaine, is on the sofa fawning over the little pink bundle cradled in her arms. Cooper's mother, Nelly, is right beside her with an almost identical package. The scent of baby lotion fills my nose as I lean in to kiss their little foreheads on my way over to squeeze my bestie. "You look beautiful, Spence. How are you feeling?"

"Amazing and awful and tired. But mostly wonderful." She is glowing, despite the dark circles beneath her eyes.

"Savage, my man!" Cooper calls out, rising from the recliner that is tucked away in the corner beside the bed. He's absolutely beaming, every bit the proud papa.

"Hey, Daddy. Did you misseded me?"

"Sure did." He makes his way around the small hospital room to grab Kyle's hand and leads the three boys over to the little blue pull-out couch, where their grandmothers ooh and ahh over the twins. "Boys, meet your sisters, Abigail and Emmaline."

As I sit on the edge of my best friend's bed, taking in the boys' first reactions to the new babies, I feel her cold hand clutch mine and squeeze. My heart flips in my chest. She deserves this life—this family, this happiness—more than anyone.

"What do you think, buddy?" Spencer asks as I help Kyle up onto the bed to sit beside her.

"Be careful, Savage," I warn. "Mommy's tummy has a big

owie from getting the babies out."

"I think they're all right, but I still wish they were some boy babies instead. I saw some in that big window when we were looking for your room, Mommy." Kyle's eyes grow round. "Maybe someone else wanted girl ones and we can trade?"

"Oh, baby. Don't make me laugh right now. It hurts," she says through a strained giggle. "We're not trading your sisters in. You and your brothers...*and* your father are more than enough boy for one family."

Kyle's shoulders sag. "Fine. But you have to promise me you won't let any more guys shoot sperms in your vagima, okay?"

Spencer's eyes widen, and dart around the room until they land on Lake and Landon. "What did you two say to my baby?"

Oh, shit.

"Don't look at us," Landon laughs, throwing his hands up in surrender. "That's all Aunt Gigi's doing."

Gulp. "Oh, you two helped just a little." Look at them throwing me right under the fucking bus.

"Gina!" Mrs. Nelly gasps. "He's only four."

Cooper's face is damn near purple he's laughing so hard, and Spencer looks as though she may never speak to me again.

Sliding out of the bed slowly, I begin moving toward the door. "And that's our cue to leave. Come on boys. Kiss everyone bye. I have a big surprise for you." They don't know it yet, but when we leave this hospital, we're going straight to the Port of New Orleans to board a cruise ship headed to the Caribbean for a week. I thought it would be nice to do something fun for them while the new babies are soaking up all of the attention. Not to mention the fact that Cooper and Spencer could use the time acclimating to life with twin newborns.

That's right. This heart is made of gold. It's this mouth that keeps my ass in trouble.

"On second thought," Spencer starts, fidgeting nervously in the bed. "Maybe this surprise isn't such a good idea..."

Oh, hell no.

Mrs. Elaine shoots her daughter a sideways glance. "Spencer Rose, really? Stop it. You act like you haven't known Gina your entire life. Now, I told you one day all those baby daddies would catch up to you. Well, here you go." She waves her arms around the room.

"Uh, I'm just gonna go out and have a smoke," Cooper's father, Mr. Neal, announces before scurrying around me and out of the room.

"Mother! She's had them alone for a day. One. Day. And look what she's done. Imagine the damage she can do in a week."

Elaine simply waves her off. "She can't do anything worse than what you've already done, darlin'." After passing the baby off to Cooper she joins me near the door and leans in to whisper into my ear. "Ignore her. Just take the kids and run, baby girl. Y'all have a great time." She presses a kiss to my cheek, rolling her eyes at her daughter who's still ranting in the hospital bed.

"Did she just call me a bad mother?" Spencer's hand flies to her chest as she looks to Cooper, who suddenly appears to have seen a ghost.

"Nuh-unh. Don't involve me in y'all's—"

"So, you agree with her?"

Oh, dear God in heaven. This must be the leftover pregnancy hormones. While Coop reassures his wife that she's the most wonderful mom to ever walk this earth, I instruct the boys to say their goodbyes and meet me in the hall.

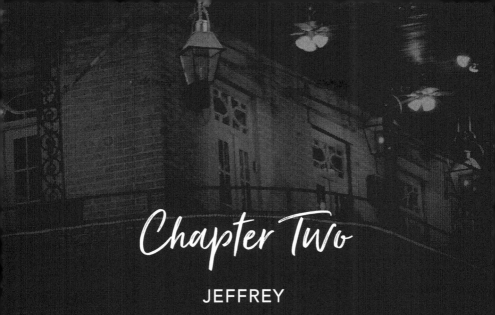

Chapter Two

JEFFREY

"You girls all packed and ready to go?"

My baby girl, Willow, comes bounding down the stairs, her blonde ringlets bouncing with each step. "I tan't wait to get on the big ship, Daddy!" At three years old, she still looks at me like I hung the moon.

"I can't believe you're making me go on this trip without Savana." As for *this* one, and her teenage drama, it seems nothing I ever do is good enough.

"It's a family vacation, Evangeline. Savana is not a part of this family."

"She's close enough." Her big emerald eyes—her mother's eyes—roll up in her head as she twirls a lock of auburn hair around her pointer finger.

"Our family consists of you, me, and Willow."

"Yeah, well, this family stinks. So, there! If Mom were still alive, she'd understand. She'd let me bring a friend, or at the very least my phone!"

A knot forms right in the center of my chest. I try not

sound exasperated with her when I clear my throat and reply. "Well, we don't know what your mother would do, honey, because she's not here anymore, and I'm doing the best I can."

"How is taking me away from my best friend and cutting me off from the rest of the world for seven whole days the best you can do, Dad?" Her eyes well up, her frustration threatening to spill over.

Times like this I really miss my wife. She would know what to do. How to handle the hormonal mess that is our daughter. Wrapping my arm around Vangie's stiff shoulders, I pull her close and kiss the top of her head. "It's one week, baby girl. It's not the end of the world, I promise. Now get your things and try not to be miserable, huh?"

"Isn't this nice?" I nudge Evangeline with my elbow, smiling down at her as we watch the ship leave the dock from the deck of our balcony suite.

My daughter shrugs her shoulders, but I catch a hint of a smile out of the corner of my eye, and I know that she's already beginning to get over her upset.

"You look just like her at your age, you know?" The words slip out of my mouth without thought. I try not to mention her too often, but in reality, I probably don't talk about her enough.

At that she smiles. "I miss her so much, Daddy."

I thought that losing Jessica would be the hardest thing I'd ever have to endure, but I was wrong. It's watching my girls grow up without her that kills me a little more each day. And it's hardest with Evangeline, because she was old enough to know everything she lost. "I do, too, Vange."

"I'm sorry I was being a brat before we left," she offers, cuddling into my side.

"Meh, don't worry about it...I'm used to it."

She lets out an indignant squeal, and all is right in my world. Or as right as it can be without our missing piece.

"Time to party, people," our cruise director Stan shouts, clapping the mic in his hands as he stands on the stage in the center of the main deck.

"Why dat man wearin' a skirt?" Willow giggles.

"It's called a kilt," her sister snaps with a roll of her eyes.

"Well, why dat man wearin' a tilt?"

"It's a boy skirt," I whisper into my little girl's ear.

"In Scotland," Vangie starts, before realizing it's too difficult to explain to a toddler, "never mind."

"Come on," I say, lifting Willow up onto my shoulders and moving toward the dance floor before Evangeline has the chance to refuse. There's no way she'll stay back alone. "Time for some line dancing!"

"Oh, my God, Dad. Since when do you line dance?"

Looking back over my shoulder, I smirk at the look of annoyance on her face. "Since right now."

Vangie falls in line beside me, dancing like a pro while I stumble through the moves. "This is so embarrassing," she complains, but her beaming face tells a different story.

"Lighten up. No one here knows you. There's freedom in anonymity. Enjoy it."

I can't believe the things I find myself doing just to see these girls smile.

Chapter Three

GINA

Ahhh. This is the life. I don't know why Spencer was going on and on about vacation with kids not being relaxing. That bitch just isn't taking the right vacations. Auntie Gina is gonna have to show her how it's done.

"Thank you, Philip." I smile sweetly at the little Cuban guy who keeps bringing me fresh drinks. The staff on this ship take customer service to a whole other level. Before I even realize I need something, someone is already taking care of it.

I do find it odd, however, that their nationalities are etched above the names on their badges, and can't help but think of the discrimination lawsuits that would bring on in America. As a matter of fact, I don't think I've seen a single American employee. I couldn't begin to imagine having to serve other people for a living, but everyone here is so accommodating. They really seem to enjoy their jobs, so it's probably for the best.

"See you in a few minutes, Phil!" I call after him as he heads off in the direction of the bar. Then, I grab my phone and flip the camera to selfie mode.

With my free hand I fluff up the blonde hair at the crown of my head to give it more volume. Then I adjust the girls in my hot pink bikini top, grab my daiquiri from the little side table, flash my pearly whites, and *snap.*

Me: Morning bestie! How are you and my baby girls feeling? Y'all blow that joint yet?

Spencer: Hey hooker. Not yet. They said maybe tomorrow.

Her reply is almost instant. She must be bored out of her mind, so I attach the selfie to my response in an attempt to make her feel worse about her situation. I'm a good friend like that.

Me: That's a shame. Really wish you could be here relaxing with me.

Spencer: Are you slutting it up with my kids, Gina?

Me: Built in babysitters, biotch! We spent a few hours together at the pool, had lunch, then I shipped their asses off to the kid rooms 'til dinner.

Spencer: Just don't get too drunk, and make sure they don't like get too close to the edge of the boat. How's Savage? Is he seasick? Does he love it?

Me: Calm your tits, woman. We're fine. Everyone is fine. They're loving it! Go enjoy those babies. I'm gonna catch a little sun. Love you, bestie.

Just as I go to set my phone down it dings. *Spencer really needs to learn to let go a little,* I think as I bring the phone back to my face.

Aaaand I was wrong. It's Brent. Stage five clinger.

Brent: Hey doll face. Wanna come over to my place? Netflix and chill?

My eyes roll up into the back of my head. *Netflix and chill?* Gross.

Now, don't get me wrong, I'm used to the millennial lingo and the overall douchiness that goes along with dating younger guys, but Brent just...he doesn't know when to quit.

Me: I'm on vacation with my godsons. Sorry.

Brent: Awe, bummer. Another time then? When do you get back?

Me: Yeah. I don't think that's gonna happen, Brent. A one-night stand with me consists literally of one night.

Brent: All right well...you have a great vacation and maybe we can get together when you get back?

It's not often I can't shake a guy. I've pretty much narrowed my selection process down to a science, and Brent fits the bill perfectly. Early to mid-twenties, check. Gym junkie, check— I've found men obsessed with working out don't have much time for anything else, making them ideal for me. College student, check. Manwhore, check.

And then there are my own personal preferences: dark hair, tanned skin, eyes the color of whiskey...So, I'm a bit of a *doppelbanger*. An image of William Levy floats across the backs of my eyelids, and I press my thighs together. Something about that man in those telenovelas just does it for me. I'd add the ability to dirty talk in Español to my list if I didn't live in one of the least diverse towns in America.

My skin heats beneath the sun's rays, and I'm finally beginning to doze off when I feel a finger tapping my shoulder.

Pushing my sunglasses up, I have to squint to make out Landon's face. *How long have I been out?* With a quick glance down at my phone, I realize it's only two-thirty. "Miss me already, Lan?"

"Uhh," he mumbles. The shakiness of his voice has me bolting straight up to a sitting position.

Before I even get the chance to ask him what's going on, I hear a throat clear, pulling my attention to the man and young girl who are standing behind him.

"Can I help you?" My adrenaline starts pumping, going into defense mode as I return his stare.

"Son," he says, addressing Landon instead of me, "I asked you to take me to your parents, not your sister. I haven't got time for this." His crystal blue eyes narrow.

Who the fuck does this man think he is, talking to Landon like that?

"Sir, she is my...uh—"

"Excuse me," I interject, cutting him off, "Landon is my nephew, and I'm the one responsible for him this week, so if you need to speak to his parent, 'fraid I'm it."

A slight blush creeps across the man's stony face. His features are hard, his jaw ticking. "I just caught your nephew kissing my daughter on the main deck."

My hands curl at my sides as I draw in a deep breath, resisting the urge to squeal. "Like with tongue?" I blurt out, slapping a hand over my mouth. I can hardly contain my excitement. *Oh. My. God.* My boy is growing up...

Landon hangs his head in embarrassment as the angry man with the bluest eyes and most amazing blond hair I've ever seen begins breathing so hard I practically expect fire to shoot out from his flared nostrils. "I'm pretty sure tongues were involved," he answers with a curt nod. His arms cross on his chest as he awaits my response.

"Way to go Landon!" I shout, wrapping my bony arms around him in a bear hug and rocking from side to side. "We should celebrate! You just had your first kiss...That *was* your first one right?"

"Aunt Gina..." he mutters beneath his breath. His eyes gesturing to the grumbly man behind him.

"Celebrating is not exactly what I had in mind." The girl's father gives her a stern look when a giggle, despite her best efforts to hold it in, escapes her pressed lips.

Giving the flustered little redhead a wink, I rise to my feet, putting myself on more even ground, although he still stands at least a foot taller than my five-foot frame. "And just what did you have in mind Mr....?" I trail off, waiting for him to find his manners and actually introduce himself.

His hand reaches out for mine. "Jeffrey Ryan, CEO of Ryan Drilling."

Sucking in my cheeks, I try really hard not to laugh at how proud he is of his title. Well, I'm just as proud of my own. "Gina Bourque," I return, giving his hand a shake. "Sex therapist."

Chapter Four

JEFFREY

Sex thera—. Well, there went any hopes I had of parental support. Looks like it'll be up to me alone to keep that kid's grubby paws off my daughter.

"And what's your name, gorgeous?" Tinkerbell asks, withdrawing her tiny hand from mine and reaching out for my little girl's.

"Evangeline."

"That's such a pretty name. Y'all have got to be from Louisiana, too, with a name like Evangeline?"

What is it with this woman acting like we're all pals? I came here looking for some assistance in keeping these two apart, not to help them get to know one another better. And why is she looking at me like she's hiding some dirty secret? More importantly, why am I so curious?

"My parents are from a town called Catahoula, but we live about an hour from New Orleans in Livingston." Vangie flips her hair dramatically, an obvious move for that boy's attention.

"Ah, I know just where you're talking about. I used to work

in New Orleans, and Landon here lived there his whole life, until we all moved back to Cedar Grove the year before last. Right, Lan?" Gina, the *sex therapist*, nudges the little punk with her elbow, trying to include him in the conversation.

Evangeline's face turns somber, and my heart grows tight inside of my chest because I know what's coming. "Well, we used to live in Catahoula until Mom died. We've only been in Livingston about three years."

Gina reaches out a hand, smoothing down my daughter's hair in an affectionate manner—the way a mother would. I don't know why that bothers me so much, but I don't like seeing another woman in Jessica's place. This is stupid. She's a stranger. She is nothing to me. "I'm sorry about your mom, sweetie."

Shaking myself from a daze, I clear my throat. "All right, well—it was nice meeting y'all. If you could encourage Landon here to keep away from my daughter, I'd appreciate it." Grabbing Vangie's hand, I begin to move away when I feel someone take hold of my other arm.

"Jeffrey?" The petite blonde calls in a warm, raspy voice that sounds far too mature for her tiny frame and youthful face. She pulls in close, her hand resting on the front of my T-shirt, causing my heart to drum in my chest. She rises to her tippy toes, breathing hot on my ear. Making sure not to let the children hear, she whispers, "I can see you're having issues with this."

I grunt in response, trying not to react to her nearness. To the smell of strawberries and coconuts that are engulfing my senses.

"But, there is nothing you or I am going to do that's going to keep these two apart, short of locking them in our cabins for the duration of the trip..."

"Please, Tinkerbell—"

Her eyes widen at my slip of the nickname I've been calling her in my head.

"Don't think I'm not considering doing just that."

"Do you want to make her hate you?" Her warm fingers tighten around my bicep. "Because I can tell you that's exactly what you're going to do if you continue treating her this way. I can see that you don't like me. That's okay. To be completely honest, I don't like you either. But, Landon means the world to me. He is a good kid. You couldn't ask for better for your daughter's first crush. The way I see it, we've got two options. We can either choose to explore this thing with them, together. Or, forbid them, and they'll sneak around. Hell, even if they don't...Do you think your daughter will ever tell you about her personal life if this is the expectation you've set?"

My tongue rolls across my front teeth, and I swallow a lump of pride, because as much as I hate to admit it, she's right. Jessica and I began seeing each other when she was exactly her age. "You may have a point," I concede.

She winks a triumphant green eye at me, before stepping back and announcing to the children with a clap of her hands, "Looks like Jeffrey and Evangeline have decided to join us at the pool 'til dinner."

Evangeline looks up at me, so hopeful. With a resigned sigh, I wave her off. "Go ahead but stay by the pool where we can see you, and no more kissing." My eyes narrow at the boy whose cheeks redden.

"Yes, sir," he nods, grabs my daughter's hand, and the two of them scramble off to the other end of the pool.

"Good job, Daddy," she clamps me on the lower back. "Why don't you scowl at the children from that chair right there?" She points to the one on the other side of the little table that houses her drink, rather than the one right beside her. Holding up her frozen concoction, she swirls it in the air. "Phil makes a mean strawberry daiquiri."

"This is a family vacation. I don't drink when I'm with my girls."

Her tiny shoulders shrug, and she gives me a sympathetic smile. "Sucks to be you."

Reluctantly, I plant my ass in the lounger, with every intention of stewing in silence, but that intrusive little blonde has other ideas.

"So, Jeffrey," she says after sipping from her fruity drink. "What do you like to do for fun?"

Is she serious right now? "Look, Gina, don't feel like you need to make small talk, okay? I'm perfectly fine to just sit here and keep watch."

"Fine," she pouts. Actually pouts—like a child. I can't believe someone entrusted this tart with the well-being of her children.

"Well, that's boring."

"I like boring," I assure her, trying not to stare as she reapplies tanning oil to her perky little breasts, humming along to the music that's blaring from the speakers surrounding the deck. My dick stirs. I'm attracted to her, and that's pissing me off too.

"I must say that I'm surprised, Jeff. You don't look like a stiff." Her eyes meet mine, issuing a challenge.

Why won't this chick just leave me alone? "Trust me," I say, glaring in her direction. "I'm stiff." Much to my dismay.

"So *that's* your problem." She nods her head as if she's just figured me all out. She has no fucking clue. "Been a while?"

"Forward much?"

Again, she shrugs. "It's the therapist in me. I'm psychoanalyzing you. Does that bother you, Jeffrey?"

"You bother me."

"I can tell." This girl actually has the audacity to look to my lap. My dick twitches, hardening beneath her gaze.

Gina's lips curl into a knowing smile. "You're not my usual type, but I must say you've piqued my interest. How long's it been?"

"Are you seriously asking that question to a complete stranger?"

"Why not? We're adults. Does talking about sex make you uncomfortable?"

She's got to be fucking with me. "You're something else, you know that?" I ask, laughing her off.

"I've been told," Tink agrees as she begins flailing her hand in the air at the cabana boy. "Bring me another, Phil?"

His head bobs, and he shoots her a thumbs-up from across the deck.

Gina flashes a blinding white smile, blowing him a kiss before spinning back around in her chair to face me. "You said you were here with your daughters...How many?"

"Two," I answer, clearing my throat. "Evangeline, who you've met, is fourteen. And the little one, Willow, is three."

"Must be hard, running a company and raising two kids on your own."

Does she have no boundaries? "I manage."

I'm caught off guard when she reaches out, patting the top of my left hand where it's resting on the arm of my chair. "You should know you're doing a good job."

"You don't even know me," I rasp, both shocked by her

nerve and at how relieved I am to hear those words.

The therapist in her must be able to read the doubt in my features. "A bad father wouldn't go after some boy for daring to kiss his baby...Or worry about drinking around his kids." She nods, mostly to herself.

Well, this got uncomfortable really quickly—not that a moment of this conversation has been remotely comfortable. "So, uh. You have any kids, Tink?"

I think I see a hint of sadness in her eyes, but it's gone so quickly that I could've imagined it altogether. "Nope," she answers, popping the p. "Just me."

"Husband or a boyfriend?" *What is wrong with me?* I don't actually care about any of this.

"Now who's being forward?" she asks, arching her brow. "No hubby and no boyfriend." Her tongue darts out to wet her lips as her eyes give me a thorough once-over. "I'm enjoying the single life entirely too much...I just borrow my bestie's kids and give 'em back when I've had my fill."

"That's probably for the best...You don't really strike me as the mothering type."

"Well, then. Maybe the man upstairs knew just what he was doing when he dealt me a bunch of faulty equipment."

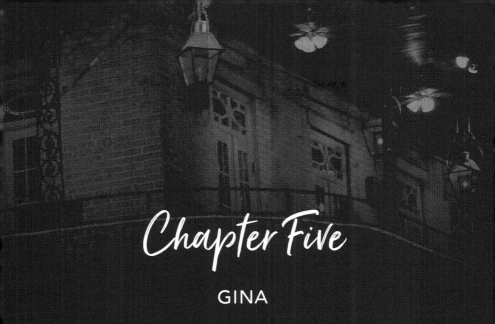

Chapter Five

GINA

"I'm sorry. I shouldn't have just assumed you didn't want children," he says, his brows dipped inward with concern. "I wish I hadn't said that."

With my best poker face, I tamp down the pesky emotions that still threaten to make an appearance now and again, forcing myself to smile. "No worries."

He starts to speak again then seems to think better of it, and his mouth clamps shut. The silence shouldn't feel this awkward between us. We hardly know each other. "Hey, Jeff?"

"Yeah, Tinkerbell?"

Why does my stomach flip when he calls me that stupid name? It's not at all original. I've been called that or "pixie" my entire life, given my small size, blonde hair, and green eyes. But when he says it, something deep inside stirs giving me a little throb between the legs—a vaginal heartbeat, if you will.

Dammit. I'm going to have to fuck him. I've never slept with an older man before. Well, I mean...he can't be all that old. But I think twenty-five has been the oldest I've been with.

Jeff *needs* me, poor man—I reason with myself. Plus, my vagina would never forgive me for not scratching this itch. And I'm finding myself very curious about his sex noises. Every time he growls, I wonder what he sounds like moaning in pleasure.

It's settled. Jeffrey and I are going to do the nasty!

"Tink?"

"Huh? Sorry, I guess I kinda got lost in my own head for a sec."

His answering laugh is hearty and rich and oh, so manly. What the hell am I doing crushing on a single dad? A fucking widow at that?

"You said my name."

"I did?"

"Yup."

Oh, yeah. "Hey, has anyone ever told you that you sort of look like Chris Hemsworth?"

"Chris Hemsworth, eh? Don't women find him kinda hot?"

Gulp. "Definitely."

"Are you saying you find me attractive, Tink?" Damn him and that fucking smirk straight to hell.

"You're not bad for an older dude."

Jeff's hand goes to his chest, "Ouch, you wound me. Just how old do you think I am?"

Eyeing him head to foot, I take in the light dusting of gray mixed in with the blond at both of his temples and in the scruff on his chin. The fine lines in the corners of his eyes, which somehow only add to his appeal. He's in great physical shape—long and lean with defined muscles. His Adam's apple, prominent in the front of his throat, makes my mouth water. "Um. I'd guess thirty-five-*ish*?"

His laughter reveals a perfect set of straight, white teeth.

"How old are you?" he counters. "That you think thirty-five is old."

This should be interesting. "How old do you think I am?" I lift my brow, crossing my arms on my chest. It doesn't escape my notice how his eyes zone right in on my breasts.

"Well, you look about twenty-three."

I feel heat flood my cheeks as I beam at his answer.

"That's not a compliment, by the way. I really thought you were his sister. But, having spoken to you, and since he's your friend's kid...shit. Umm. I'll go with thirty...No. Let me say twenty-nine, to be safe."

"Thirty-five," I deadpan, enjoying the look of shock on his face.

He sputters for a moment in disbelief. "How old are the guys you date?"

I give him a noncommittal shrug. "To be clear, I don't date...I *fuck*. And usually somewhere in the twenty-two to twenty-five range."

"Cougar."

Gasp. "No...I just have a thing for young, eager men. They fuck like they have something to prove, and aren't out searching for their future brides."

"Thirty-eight and you'd be amazed how much better a man gets with age." He leans back further in his chair, trailing his eyes up and down my body.

"Is that an invitation?" I ask, biting my lower lip.

"To be clear, I don't date," he answers, throwing my words back at me. "I *fuck*."

"Hey, Daddy?" Evangeline calls, jogging around to our end of the pool. Perfectly timed to save me from having to respond. Jesus, my heart is racing.

"Yeah, princess?" He called her princess. My fucking nonexistent ovaries damn near explode.

"The Scotsman just announced an '80s party out here tonight after dinner. You think maybe we could all meet up?"

Jeff looks my way in question.

"Sure. Sounds like fun."

He nods before resting his hands on his knees and rising from the lounger. "Guess we'll see y'all after dinner. It's about time for us to go get your sister from the kid room, Vange."

"Ah, Miss Gina, Lake, Landon, and you must be Kyle, the man in charge." Our server, Wesley, greets us at our table by name, placing a basket of assorted breads in the center and filling our water glasses. He's dark, Haitian per his nametag, with an exuberant smile of strikingly white teeth.

Wesley tells us that he's been working on the cruise ships for over ten years and has four boys back home and another on the way. He works six-month contracts and goes home just long enough to make another baby before he's back out to sea.

"Just freaking great!" Kyle announces, rolling his eyes.

Oh, no.

"Mr. Wesley," Kyle starts, staring the man straight in the face. "Please don't shoot your sperms in my Aunt Gigi's *vagima*. We already have too many babies."

Water sprays out from my mouth and nose as I begin choking. I swear that man's face, dark as it is, has turned ten shades of red. I can't catch my breath.

"Kyle!" Lake shouts through guffaws. "Dude, that was so rude."

The savage four-year-old's face falls. Those big brown eyes well with tears, and he becomes panicked. He really is a sweet baby.

"It's okay, Kyle," I reassure him, dabbing the tears of mirth from my eyes with my napkin. "It's just not nice to talk to strangers about their sperm, okay?" His little head nods, that signature booboo lip hanging to the floor. "Just tell Mr. Wesley you're sorry."

"I'm sorry." A big crocodile tear drips down his cheek, and I pull him into my lap, cuddling my little boyfriend. I never could handle seeing him upset.

Wesley, bless his heart, is a great sport about the whole thing. Kyle's tears have our waiter all flustered as well and earn him a cup of ice cream before dinner.

Just as Savage is finishing up his pre-dinner dessert, I hear him groan, and he hangs his head. "Oh, brudder."

"Dats Tyle! He's in my group, Daddy, and I'm going to mawwy him!" pipes a little voice from nearby.

I look to the once-empty table to the left of us, which is now occupied by none other than Mr. CEO and his two daughters. His little one is an absolute doll, with the bounciest blonde curls, her daddy's blue eyes, and dimples for days. She's his spitting image. In other words—*trouble.*

"You're not marrying anyone, Willow. You're going to live with Daddy forever," Jeffrey says to his daughter in a no-nonsense tone without the slightest hint of a smile. I do believe the man is serious.

And, he's fucking beautiful in his black button down, tucked into charcoal gray dress pants. Black shoes. Black belt. If it weren't for the tenderness he exudes with his girls, I'd swear he had a black heart to match.

"Yeah," Kyle agrees. "Listen to your dad. I'm already marrying my Aunt Gina." His declaration is loud, earning us the attention and giggles of half the dining room.

"Should have known the boy Willow hasn't stopped talking about would belong to you," Jeffrey grumbles before cracking a smile of his own.

"Can't help it that we're all so irresistible." I shrug my shoulders, and his face hardens for a moment.

"Don't flatter yourself, Tink." *Ouch.* His attention turns to his girls, and I force mine back to my godsons.

What an asshole. Ah, well. It will just make the sex that much better. I could be down with some good hate sex!

"Catch me a glow stick, Auntie Gigi!" Kyle shouts as the Scotsman and his assistants begin tossing various-sized neon glow sticks out into the crowd. Prince's "1999" has everyone bouncing on their feet, including a certain CEO who I'm doing my best to ignore. I jump as high as I can every time they come our way, but being little has its disadvantages.

Just as I'm about to go snatch one from the hand of a stranger, Jeffrey appears in front of Kyle with a huge, bright orange, glowing baton and a neon yellow necklace, which he drapes around his neck.

"There ya go, buddy."

Kyle's eyes light up. "Thank you!"

"You're welcome."

My heart thrums in my throat as I watch the two of them engaged in conversation, with Jeff crouched down to his level.

"I'm still not marrying your daughter," Kyle announces.

The CEO sucks in his cheeks and lips, warding off a smile. "That's the best news I've heard all day."

"You should really talk to her. She's kind of pushy."

"I'm trying," Jeffrey assures him. "But she pushes me around too."

Kyle nods. "Also, I think you need to tell Auntie Gigi you're sorry. You hurted her feelings when you told her not to flatter herself."

Heat radiates from my every pore as I pretend not to hear their conversation, diverting my attention off to the side where the three teenagers are bouncing around with Willow.

"That hurt her feelings, did it?"

"I think so and anyway my daddy says you should always flatter women because it makes them happy, and a happy woman will give you all the things. He says Aunt Gigi is a force, so we should all do what we can to keep her and Mommy happy."

"Well, your daddy sounds like a very intelligent man."

"He is," I hear Kyle answer before my name is yelled out in his voice, "Gigi! Come see."

I take a deep breath then turn and walk over to join them. "Yes, Kyle?"

"Mr. CEO has something he needs to say to you."

Jeff blushes. "It has come to my attention that I may have unintentionally hurt your feelings at dinner earlier tonight..."

"Please," I laugh. "Don't flatter yourself into thinking you had any effect on my feelings."

He shrugs, looking down at Kyle before rising to his feet.

"You tried." Kyle throws his hands up in defeat.

"I tried," Jeffrey echoes as Willow runs over, trying to pull Kyle out onto the dance floor.

"Tum dance wif me, husband." That sweet blonde baby yanks on my stubborn godchild's arm, and he doesn't budge. The look on his face is pure disgust. It's amazing.

"I think you might hurt her feelings if you don't go dance with her, Kyle," Jeffrey says, giving Kyle back a bit of his own advice.

Conceding with a groan, he allows the little girl to pull him away. "Women!"

Jeff chuckles, staring after them and nods in agreement. "Women!"

When the '80s party ends at 10:00 p.m., the children all beg to go back to their respective kids' clubs until they shut down at midnight. That leaves Jeff and me meandering the halls back toward the elevators, together.

Luck would have it that we end up in the same elevator, *alone*. I'm a little tipsy and a lot horny, and beyond tired of this tension. So, I decide to throw him a bone and see if he'll bite. "Is it wet in here?" I ask, nibbling my bottom lip seductively.

Jeffrey's face screws up in confusion as he looks around the elevator, finally landing on my face. "No."

"Oh, my bad. Must just be my *vagina*."

Chapter Six

JEFFREY

What in God's name is wrong with this woman?

My cock grows rigid in my suit pants as I stare at her braced against the handrail, her tongue tracing over her lips. It's pure insanity, but I want to explore this crazy world she's offering. I've never been with a woman so blunt, so uninhibited, and if I'm honest with myself, I've had a hard-on for her since the moment I saw her lounging in that scrap of a bikini on the main deck.

If she's offering...Why the hell shouldn't I indulge?

"No strings?" I ask, sauntering over and resting my hands on the railing, just outside of where hers rest.

Tink's head shakes. "Just scratching an itch, Jeffrey." The husky tone of her voice makes me throb with want.

Nodding, I bend my head to the dip between her shoulder and neck, ghosting the tip of my nose up the sensitive skin. Her perfume is soft and flowery. "Show me where you itch..." I rasp, trailing my tongue along the shell of her ear, biting down gently when I reach the lobe.

Gina grips my hand, moving it to the space between her legs. Lifting her skirt with our joined hands, she slips the bathing suit bottom to the side and pushes my index finger between her folds. "In here," she moans, writhing into my hand. Her arms reach up and around my shoulders, her hands tugging the hair at the nape of my neck.

"How's that?" I ask withdrawing my finger and reentering with two. Fuck. She's dripping.

"Deeper," she murmurs, sucking on my neck. She fists my erection, stroking through the thin material of my suit pants.

And good Lord, I'm so taken with her that I'm seconds away from whipping it out and fucking her in this elevator, but then the bell chimes as the doors start to open, and our private moment is intruded on by a gaggle of teenage girls.

Withdrawing my fingers discreetly, I ease to the side. My heart hammers against my rib cage as I try to reorient myself.

Flustered, Gina reaches around, pushing the button for the Serenity deck. *Adults only.*

When the elevator stops, I follow her out to one of the dome-shaped double loungers. The only way anyone would be able to see what's going on inside is if they were to walk around and peer in. There are a few couples lurking about, but none are paying us any mind.

"You want to do this here?" I ask, looking around, hesitant as she slips off her flip-flops and crawls in.

"I'm getting off in this little moon chair with or without your assistance, CEO. So, either get your ass in here and make yourself useful, or stand there and watch." Looking over her shoulder, she bats her long lashes up at me. Without breaking eye contact, she trails the fingers of one hand up her thigh, bringing the skirt of her dress along with it. Before she can get her hand inside her bathing suit bottom, I'm sidled up behind her, unfastening my pants.

"I don't date, Tink. Tell me you understand that." My lips are hot on her ear as I grind my erection into the small of her back.

Her body trembles against mine. "I believe we've already hashed this all out."

"I'm serious."

"So am I," she says, reaching around to palm my cock. "I don't catch feelings, Jeff. Don't even want you to be my friend."

Could it really be this easy?

Her tiny fist feels so fucking good moving up and down my shaft. "Tell me what you want."

"To use you, the same way you want to use me." Her hand tightens around my cock. "Make it good, Jeffrey."

While Tink makes quick work of my belt and zipper, I retrieve a condom from my wallet.

"Allow me," she says, snatching the foil packet from my hand and opening it with her front teeth. "I like to be the one administering my protection," she explains.

My hips jerk as she rolls the latex on. "Be my guest," I grunt, slamming into her tiny opening the second her hand is out of the way.

Gina gasps loudly in surprise. "Shhh," I whisper, nibbling on her ear, as I withdraw and thrust inside of her hard and fast.

"Yes," she moans. "Harder Jeffrey...Oh, God. It's so deep."

"Shhh," I chuckle, cupping one hand over her mouth and bringing the other around to her swollen clit. "Quiet, Tinkerbell."

She bites down on my pointer finger, moaning and jerking her hips to match my rhythm. With one hand over her shoulder she pulls my hair, holding my mouth to her neck. The other slips inside her top, to squeeze her breast.

All of the blood rushes to my dick as I pound away, sating this overwhelming lust without fear of misleading her—without the guilt that plagues me each time the mere thought of trying to move on with another woman enters my mind. There's no love between us. Zero emotion. We're satisfying a primal urge. And in this moment, it's everything I need.

"Ahh," Willow sighs dramatically, relaxing in her miniature pedicure chair. "Dis duh wife!"

"Sir," the technician, Judy, calls out, waving me over. "We have chair ready for you." Her hand waves in a Vanna White motion over the seat next to Evangeline, who is already fighting a case of the giggles as I climb in.

"Man, I wish I had my phone, so I could get a picture of you getting your nails done to send to Gramma Betty."

"Evangeline?"

"Yeah, Daddy?" she asks, still snickering.

"Keep it up and you just might not get that phone back when we get home."

"You want color?" Judy asks as she dumps blue crystals into the steaming water.

"No—"

"Him want pink powish," Willow answers, cutting me off.

Shaking my head at the woman, I mouth the word, *no*.

"Oh, come on, Dad. It's a family vacation," Evangeline reminds me. "No one knows us here, remember? Anonymity, and all that."

"You've got me in a nail salon filled with women, and I'm letting people touch my feet. I draw the line at painted toes."

"Pwease, Daddy-oh," Willow begs. "You da best daddy in da whoooole world."

The technician places a hand on her hip, looking at me expectantly. "You make your baby girl so happy, Daddy."

"Paint 'em black, to match his heart," rasps the husky voice belonging to the woman I lay awake thinking about all night. She slaps the bottle of polish she's already retrieved from the spinny thing into Judy's hand.

"Are you stalking me?" I ask, turning to find Gina smirking at me with a hand on her hip. Her blonde hair is pulled up into a knot on the top of her head and large sunglasses hide her eyes.

"You got me, Jeff. I just knew I'd wake up at the ass crack of dawn and find you in the beauty salon, getting your nails done."

"It's after ten, Tink. That's just about lunch time for most people."

She lifts her glasses up with a finger so I can see her eyes roll. "I'm not most people, Jeffrey."

"No," I agree, watching her climb up into the chair across from mine. "Thank God for that. I don't think the world could handle two of you."

Chapter Seven

GINA

"Thank you." I smile as I grab the mimosa from the procured hand of the technician who's filling my pedicure tub, beginning my attempt to drink away the looming hangover from last night's binge. As I set my glass into the cup holder, I somehow manage to lock eyes with the CEO, who just happens to be giving me a disapproving look. *Big shock there.*

Who does this man think he is? The fun police?

Focusing on my phone so I don't have to look at his stupid judgmental face, I scroll through Facebook and play a few games of Candy Crush. When what I deem to be a safe amount of time has passed, I steal another look.

Without thought, I lift my phone, snapping a picture of the tender moment between Jeffrey and his girls. Then, I stare at it, my insides twisting up into knots. His feet are resting on the ledge, where the technician is applying a second coat of Pepto pink polish to his toes. He's laughing at something one of the girls must have just said.

For a moment I forget what a jerk he is. With them, he's an absolute prince. I have no clue what happened to their mother, but I'm curious. My heart aches for their loss. There's something about seeing this man with these little girls that has my insides turning to mush.

I attach the picture with a message to my best friend.

Me: I fucked him in a moon chair on the Serenity deck last night. Do you still love me, even though I'm a bit of a ho?

Spence: Where were my kids?

Me: In the kid camps.

Spence: Then of course. Everyone should go through a ho phase. It builds character.

Me: See. This is why I love you.

After my pedicure, I retrieve the boys and take them to the buffet line for lunch. We grab a table near the windows, so we can look out at the ocean while we eat. We've barely touched our food when Jeffrey and his girls slide into the booth directly across from ours. I try to ignore the way my heart starts racing at his nearness. At the way my blood heats, remembering his thick cock slamming into me last night.

"Why don't you and Willow sit with Ms. Gina and Kyle, and the twins and I can sit at this one?" Evangeline suggests to her father, drawing me from my thoughts. My cheeks heat with shame, as if any of them has any clue what I was just daydreaming about.

"Just sit down and eat your lunch. We're not asking anyone to move." Jeff looks annoyed with life, but I'm sure it's just having to be around us—me in particular. He talks a good game, but I can already tell those girls could get him to do just about anything they wanted. The way he adores them makes him impossible for me to hate.

"We don't mind switching spots with you," Landon insists, shoving Lake out of the booth. It's so cute how eager he is to be with his girl. Spencer is going to flip when I tell her about this.

The fourteen-year-old ginger groans at Jeffrey. "You told me to try not to be miserable on this vacation, Dad. This is me...*trying*." Her eyes plead with her father's. "Can't you try too, *please*?"

Begrudgingly, he agrees. "If it's okay with Tink—er, I mean Gina."

He looks to me for permission, and our eyes lock. That damn vaginal heartbeat is back. *Thump. Thump. Thump.* "Of course we don't mind. Do we, Savage?"

"Actually—," he starts, his eyes homing in on the bubbly blonde who's already climbing into the bench seat across from him. "I don't really feel like company right now." His eyes grow wide, begging me to get rid of his unwanted stalker.

"Stop it, Kyle. Be nice." I don't tell him no often, but I will not allow him to hurt that precious little girl's feelings.

"What tolor did you get, Gigi?" the three-year-old asks, referring to my nails.

I hold my hand out in her direction. "Aqua, like the waves. What color did you decide on?"

Willow holds her hand in front of her face, wiggling her fingers. "Me and my daddy both dot pink ones!"

Jeff's head hangs, and Kyle's eyes bug out. "What kind of man are you?"

"The kind who'll do anything to make his little princess

smile."

Kyle bursts out laughing. "Sucker!"

"Tyle," Willow drawls. "You didn't even tompliment my new hairdo." She must have gotten her hair blown out after her pedicure.

"Oh, brudder." I try to contain my laughter as Savage's eyes roll dramatically. "I not your husband, Willow. That is *not* my job."

"It's neber too soon to start praticing, Tyle."

"You two sure sound like an old married couple," I tease, addressing the two little ones, who are presently glaring at each other across the table.

"Good." Willow's smile splits her face. Gosh, her dimples are the cutest thing I've ever seen.

"Where are you guys headed after lunch?" I ask. Jeffrey is staring down into his plate like it's the most interesting thing he's ever seen. It's just fried chicken and potatoes. It ain't all that special.

"Why?" he asks, looking up at me with a frown after checking to be sure the kids aren't paying us any mind. "You planning on ruining the rest of my day as well?"

What the fuck? "You're the one who turned up at the nail salon, and you came over to join us for lunch...I figured maybe you wanted to let the kids hang out." I cross my arms on my chest and harrumph. "You don't have to be an ass to me, Jeffrey," I hiss. "I already told you, I don't catch feelings. If this is how you treat other women to keep them from falling for you, feel free to tone it down. There is absolutely zero danger of that happening."

"I was getting my nails done first." He looks and sounds so ridiculous, defending his trip to the salon, that I can't help but laugh.

"The point is...I didn't go there looking for you." I glance down to his flip-flop clad foot, sticking out into the aisle. "I don't even know why I suggested the black. Pink is definitely your color."

"If you're trying to get a rise out of me, Tink, it isn't going to work."

"I'm fairly certain you and I both know that I would have no problem getting a rise out of you *if* that's what I wanted."

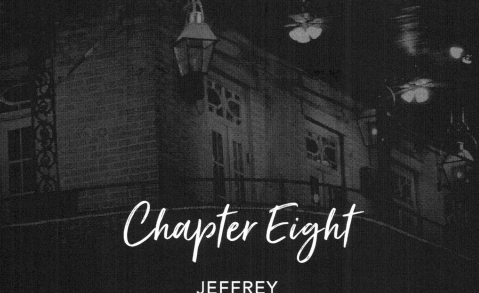

Chapter Eight

JEFFREY

It seems like everywhere I turn, Tinkerbell and those boys are there. I decided I'd take Vangie and Willow out to the main deck after nap time to see what was going on. Well, our cruise director just happened to be recruiting eight men to compete in a lip sync battle. Of course, Evangeline insisted I volunteer. No biggie. I'm not a shy guy in any sense of the word.

What I wasn't banking on was them dressing us in women's clothing. Or that, as I find myself about to take my turn down the runway in three-inch heels, wearing a red robe and hot pink feathered boa, Tink would be sitting front and center, sipping on another frozen drink. Vangie and Willow must've spotted them while I was being made into a drag queen, because they're sitting at the foot of Savage's lounge chair, staring right at me.

"Ladies and gents have we got a treat for you. Up next is Mr. Jeff Ryannnn bringing you his rendition of "Supermodel (You Better Work)" by none other than RuPaul!"

As the music starts up, I block them out, concentrating on my moves, the lyrics, and not falling on my face. *How the hell do women walk in these things?*

"Woooo! That's right, Mr. Ryan. Work it, girl! Just like that," Stan, the cruise director encourages.

When I reach the front of the catwalk, he comes over the mic again. "Now, give 'em a good twirl."

At this point, all I can hear are the faint cheers of the crowd and my own heartbeats pounding in my ears. It's almost over. Time for my big finish.

Gripping the ends of the boa in each of my hands, I play to the crowd, giving them a little shimmy while spinning in my stilettos. The tip of one of my heels catches in between the slats of wood on the deck, and my life flashes before my eyes. I fall forward, in what feels like slow motion, landing with my face right in the lap of an older gentleman sporting a bright blue Speedo.

To make matters worse—you mean it actually gets worse than a face full of wrinkled, hairy balls? Yes. Yes, it does, because I can't get up. Blinding pain shoots up my leg from my rolled ankle.

The man who I've just inadvertently assaulted helps me out of his crotch with the assistance of the intrusive blonde who I've been trying so hard to avoid.

I'm unreasonably pissed that she's taking it upon herself to make sure that I'm okay, giving up her chair, fawning all over me. I don't want to be taken care of by a woman, especially not one I'm fucking. That was my Jessica's job. It's too intimate, and it's messing with me bad.

"You otay, Daddy?" Willow asks, patting my cheeks with her chubby little hands as she climbs over the arm of the chair and into my lap. Instantly some of my ire cools as I breathe in the scent of her watermelon shampoo, taking in the look of concern in her eyes.

"That was amazing, Dad!" Evangeline gushes while Tink fusses over my hurt ankle, and I fight the urge to yank it away. "Landon got the whole thing on video. He's gonna email it to me from his phone." *Brilliant.*

The more Gina touches, the worse it hurts. It's getting hard to maintain a straight face. "Stop that," I hiss, shooing her off me. "It's fine. Just get me some ice."

Gina's eyes narrow at the bite in my tone, and she sends me a sideways glance. "You could say please, asshole."

"Ooooh," Willow howls. "Gigi just saided a bad word..." A few more days around this woman, and my girls will go home speaking like pirates.

"Please, Gina, could you get me some ice?" I grit through a pained smile.

"Certainly." She rises to her feet and begins walking toward the entrance to the buffet when I call her back.

"Tink!"

"Yeah?" she calls, looking back at me over her shoulder.

"Please watch your language around my children."

Her head spins back around, and she raises her arm into the air with the middle finger extended.

"What's dat mean, Daddy?" Willow asks, mimicking her new idol.

I clamp her little hand in mine, pushing her finger down. "Ladies don't do that, Willow. It means a very bad word."

"He means the f-you word, Willow."

"What's f-you?"

"Fuck you," Savage whisper-shouts with his hands cupped around his mouth, shocking me speechless. "Mommy says it's a grown-up sentence hancer, and you can't say dose 'til you're big."

Sentence enhancers. Dear Lord. Who *are* these people?

"Big people shouldn't be using that language around children, Kyle."

He shrugs his sun-kissed shoulders at me. "Dats what my dad says too. But, he gived up on Auntie Gigi. Her's a lost cause."

I watch the tiny blonde sashay her way back from the kitchens with the ice pack extended out in front of her—her imaginary dance partner. *How can someone so small and so unhinged be so fucking sexy?* I feel the need to bolt any time she's near, but we're stuck together for the duration of this cruise, and it doesn't seem like the girls are going to allow me to avoid her.

After icing my ankle for half an hour, I try to stand, but it's still too sore. Stan has the staff bring a wheelchair for me to get around in for the time being. Gina insists on rolling me over to the kids' camps to sign Willow in for the afternoon. At first, I refuse, but the girls start pouting, and I don't want to ruin their day just because I'm hurt, so I concede.

"You can put my name down so I can sign her in and out with Savage, if you want, then you won't have to come up before dinner and bring her back afterward."

"No offense, Tink, but I can handle things just fine on my own."

She nods, digging a prescription pad from her purse. I strain to see what she's writing on the counter above my head, but it's no use. I can't see without standing, and I won't make it obvious that I care. Because I don't... "Where'd you get a prescription pad?" The thought of this loon doling out medications is frightening.

Without looking my way, she continues scribbling as she answers. "I'm a psychiatrist, Jeffrey." Gina caps the pen, dropping it back into her purse, turns my way, and winks. "Sex is just my specialty."

My dick strains against my zipper as she leans in close, handing me the folded script. Her tits are right under my nose. I want to cup them in my hands and lick the exposed skin.

"Thanks for the orgasm," she whispers, before relinquishing her hold on the slip of paper. Gina backs a few steps away, lifting her fingers to her plump lips. With her eyes fixed on mine, she presses a long, slow kiss to the tips and blows. "See ya 'round, Jeff."

Her ass moves from side to side in those little hot pink booty shorts as she walks away with purpose.

Ask and you shall receive.

I'm equal parts pissed at her for leaving me to fend for myself, even if it is exactly what I told her to do, and turned on at her nerve.

When she's disappeared from sight, I unfold the sheet clasped in my hand.

Orgasms, take for pain as needed. Room 436.

Chapter Nine

GINA

I abandoned Jeff at the Little Fish camp over an hour ago with an invitation to the party that's about to go down in my vag. *He's still not here.* The man infuriates me with his holier-than-thou attitude, but dear Lord, that dick is huge. His cock alone is almost enough to make me forgive him for being a total asshole. I'm just about to give up and pull out my bullet when there's a knock at the door. *Finally.* Butterflies run rampant in my tummy at the anticipation.

Jumping up from the couch, I rush over to the mirror and plump up the girls in my suit top. I pull my mesh cover up over to one side, exposing one shoulder and a fair amount of cleavage before pulling the door open to find Mr. CEO smirking up at me from his chair. There's a light sheen of sweat across his forehead, no doubt from the exertion it took to wheel himself all over the damn ship. Serves him right. His hair is mussed, a few strands sticking to the skin along his hairline. His white V-neck fits his lean muscled chest to perfection, and judging by the bulge in his khaki cargo shorts, he's just as eager for round two as I am.

A deep throaty laugh draws me from my visual assault. "You gonna invite me in, Tink? Or did you really invite me over here so you could eye fuck me in the hall?" He peers around my body, appraising his surroundings. "I'm told this is the place for medically prescribed orgasms?" He quirks his left brow, pulling his lower lip between a set of perfectly white, perfectly straight teeth.

Why's he have to be so fucking gorgeous?

"Didn't think you'd come," I admit, moving into the doorway of the small bathroom, allowing enough space for him to enter the room. His chair just barely fits between the set of bunk beds on the left and the closet on the right.

"Doctor's orders." Jeff shrugs his shoulders as he stands from the wheelchair, bracing most of his weight on his good leg.

The front of my body brushes his as I scoot past him to stand in front of the queen-sized bed in the center of the room. The contact has my already eager body going haywire. "Thought you weren't the kind of man to take orders."

Another half-smile. "Only those that suit me."

The ship jerks, and my tummy does a little flip. "Are you saying that I suit you, Jeffrey?"

He hobbles over to stand before me. "I think we established last night that your pussy—" he cups my sex, leaning in so close that I can feel his warm breath on my neck—"suits my dick just fine." Heat floods my core as he grips two handfuls of my long blonde locks, turning my face up to meet his. "Am I mistaken?"

I clear my throat and straighten my stance, evening out my breathing to the best of my ability. The last thing I need is this cocky man thinking he's got the upper hand. Which he may very well have...he just doesn't need to know it. "I think you should thank God every night that he gave you one redeeming quality." Smiling sweetly at the man who I am just barely not ravishing, I trail my finger along the impressive bulge in his pants.

Jeff laughs, loudly. His whole face lights up, and I feel the sound rumble deep in my belly. "Are you saying my dick is my only redeeming quality?"

"That...and these little lines right here." Lifting up to my toes, I touch a finger to the tiny creases that appear in the corners of his eyes when he smiles. My breath hitches when he melts into my touch. "These are kind of nice too," I admit, my voice hoarse.

Jeffrey wraps a hand around my waist, pulling me flush against his hard chest. "You like my wrinkles, Tink?"

"Ju—just those three." Who am I right now, and did I really just admit to being attracted to wrinkles of all things? Ew.

He nods. "Got it. I'll make sure to tell them to leave just the three when I venture into the world of Botox."

That comment causes me to giggle. After having met up with him getting his nails done, I can easily visualize it: Jeffrey sitting in the dermatologist's chair, getting injections. "Don't," I finally manage to wheeze out.

"Don't what?"

"Don't let anyone mess with your face."

He gives me a knowing look. "You like my face too, then... seems like I have a whole lot more than one redeeming quality to be grateful for."

"Don't get carried away, Casanova. Your looks are the only thing you have going for you."

"Is that right?" he asks.

"I don't know if anyone's ever told you this, Jeffrey, but your personality leaves a lot to be desired."

"Does it?" he clips, running his hands up my bare back along the inside of my coverup.

A chill ripples through me at the intimate touch. "You're a bit of an asshole."

"That's still two."

"Huh?"

"Don't tell me you forgot about king dong." He pushes his hips forward, digging the steel rod in his shorts into my belly button.

How could I forget? "Right," I groan, reaching between us to unfasten his button and zipper. "Mustn't forget that." Dropping to my knees, I slide his shorts down, past his hips, freeing what has to be nearly nine inches of man meat. Now, I've seen a lot of dick in my day and am not too easily impressed, but this has to be a near-perfect specimen. Long and thick. Neatly trimmed. My mouth actually salivates at the thought of wrapping my lips around his girth.

"Fuck, yes," he groans as I run my tongue from base to tip. He braces himself with one hand on the vanity top behind him and fists the other into my hair, slowly guiding my movements.

"Mmmm," I moan, getting turned on by the little noises coming from the back of his throat, by the feel of him growing impossibly harder beneath my skilled moves, knowing that I am the cause of his weak knees and grunts.

I'm really getting into it, sucking him hard, while taking him all the way down my throat, when the boat shifts. My usual nonexistent gag reflex cannot compete with the weak stomach I've been fighting all day and it happens: bright pink, rancid strawberry puke all over his beautiful cock.

"Holy shit!" Jeff shouts, backing out of my mouth.

"I'm so sorry," I choke out as I reach for the shirt I slept in last night that's lying on the floor by the side of the bed to wipe my mouth and nose. The alcohol burns so bad, and I can't stop gagging. "It's not you."

Before Jeffrey has the chance to react, the intercom system beeps. "Medical response team please report to room #628."

"Goddamn it! That's my room." He starts scrambling to pull up his vomit covered clothes without wasting a single second for clean-up. "The kids..."

And then it dawns on me. The older kids can check themselves out of camp. What if something happened to them? "Get in your chair, Jeffrey."

Like a madwoman I sprint down the halls as fast as I can pushing a man twice my size in a wheelchair, probably bowling over a few unassuming passengers in the process. They should have put a horn on that thing. "What if something happened to Vangie?"

The sick look on his face brings tears to my eyes. For such a surly man, he is an amazing father. I don't know what to say, so I just rub his shoulders as we wait for the elevator to stop at his floor.

When we reach his room, there are already medical personnel inside. We can't even see past the doorway to figure out what the hell is happening. "Excuse me," Jeffrey barks. "This is my room. What's going on?"

"Are you okay, Daddy?" Evangeline and Landon come running from the direction of the elevators, with Lake on their heels. "I heard them page the medics to our room."

The staff members come pouring out of the room with looks of confusion. "Is this your cabin, sir?" one confirms with Jeffrey.

"Yes. What the hell's going on?" Patience is obviously not one of his virtues.

"We were paged for a medical emergency to this room, but there's no one here. I apologize. They must have gotten the cabin number wrong."

Jeffrey jumps up out of his chair, ready to unleash his wrath on the poor workers who were only doing their job. He's understandably upset, but not thinking rationally.

"It's okay." I interject. "We were just worried about the kids, is all. I hope whoever really needs you is okay."

"What's all over your pants?" Evangeline asks her father as I push down on his shoulders, forcing him back into his chair.

Jeffrey's face turns beet red. His breathing is panicked. My evil side wants to wait and see what excuse he comes up with, but I decide the asshole has been through enough trauma for one day and come to his rescue. After all, I did just throw up all over his dick.

"He got seasick and vomited. I was helping him back to the room when we heard the page and came running."

Vangie and the twins look at the crippled CEO and smirk.

"Well, he didn't run. I ran. Like a bat out of fucking hell."

"Language, Tink!" Jeffrey bellows, taking his frustration out on me.

"Oh, shut it."

"Wait," Lake says with a puzzled look on his face. "Why were you two together? I thought you hated each other." *Perceptive little shit.*

"We do," Jeff insists. "She's infuriatingly overbearing. How do you kids stand it?"

Evangeline huffs in frustration. "God, Daddy. Do you have to be so mean? She's helping you and you're just...you're just *rude!*"

He gets a pained look on his face, pulling his lips into a flat line. "You're right, Vangie." He turns to me and gives a half-assed apology before motioning for his daughter to go ahead of him into the room. "I'm gonna go get cleaned up. We'll see you later," he says, dismissing me and the boys.

"You sure you don't need some help with that mess?" I offer, enjoying his discomfort a little more than I should be.

"No," he growls. "You've done quite enough."

"Great. After all of this, I think I need a drink."

Jeff looks down into his lap and dry heaves. "I'm pretty sure that's the last thing you need."

After stopping at one of the bars for a cocktail—because he's not my fucking boss—the boys and I go back to the room to get ready for dinner. When I push the door open, the twins' noses crinkle in disgust.

"Oh my God," Lake groans, walking into the room. "What died in here?"

Oh, shit.

"Gigi..." Landon says, suspicion coloring his tone. "Did the CEO get sick in *our* room?"

Holding their noses, the boys look around at the evidence all over the carpet in front of the vanity and on my sleep shirt.

I'm not about to tell these kids I puked on his fucking dick. "Yes. Okay. Don't tell Vangie." I eye Landon, who's sporting an evil smirk. "I mean it. Jeffrey already can't stand me."

"He can't stand you so much that you two were hanging out in our room together?" Landon asks.

"Near your bed..." Lake adds.

I cross my arms on my chest, looking up at the ceiling and around the room. "Anywhere in the cabin is near the bed, smart ass."

"I'm sure you two were what? Playing cards?" I want to slap that smirk right off Lake's face.

"Exactly," I agree.

Landon hangs his head, laughing as he echoes my lie. "Exactly."

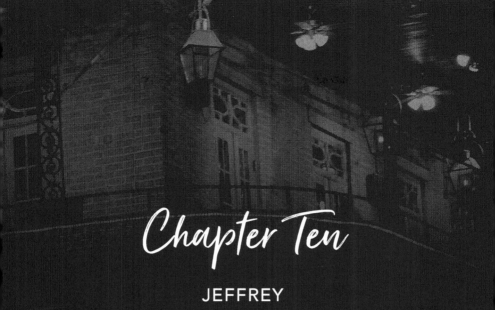

Chapter Ten

JEFFREY

Well, that was a first. I've had girls gag on my junk, sure. But, projectile vomit? Never. I pretended to still be seasick last night in order to avoid running into Tink and the boys in the dining room, opting to order room service for dinner instead.

Today we're docked in Cozumel and while I'm still limping a bit, my ankle feels a million times better. It's our first excursion, and I know, thanks to Vangie's constant whining, that her little boyfriend and posse will not be accompanying us to swim with the dolphins. I'm looking forward to a little one-on-one time with my girls.

We get off the ship and hail a cab to our excursion site, Chankanaab Park, where I booked the royal swim package, allowing us the most time with the animals. The one thing Evangeline asked for on this trip was to be able to swim with dolphins. She's been obsessed with them from the time she was around Willow's age. I can't wait to see the look on her face when she finally gets to touch one.

After fitting us into life vests, our guide Mary leads us, along with five others, to a fenced-off area in the ocean. The water is the bluest I've ever seen and surprisingly warm.

"All right guys," our guide announces, garnering the attention of our group of eight. "When it's your turn, you're going to stand like this with your arms straight out to either side of your body." As soon as she does this, two dorsal fins pop up right beneath her hands. And when she closes her fingers around them, the dolphins—Ana and Christian—take off, pulling her along for the ride.

"My turn," Willow squeals, making grabby hands for the amazing creatures.

Being the baby of the group gets her preferential treatment. Immediately, everyone looks to me, nodding their approval at allowing her to be first.

"Put your hands out just like the lady did and hold on tight," I whisper into my baby's ear as I pass her over to Mary.

She pulls her just far enough out that I can't hear what they're saying, but there is no missing the high-pitched scream and the laugh that follows when they take off.

A hand tightens around my arm and I look down to find Evangeline with the biggest and most genuine smile I think I've ever seen. "Oh my God, Dad. I'm about to ride a dolphin!"

"Two actually. Who's the best daddy in the whole world?" I gloat, puffing up with pride. Hey, I spent a lot of damn money to make her dreams come true. I want my praises.

"You always were...even before this," my sweet girl says. "But this is *so* cool. I might even clean my room to repay you." She winks and I snort. You can't even walk in that room. It's an ongoing battle, and I know damn well she's not cleaning it when we return from vacation. She'll find some reason to hate me again by then.

"Are you ready?" Mary asks Vangie after passing Willow back to me. Her arms are like a boa constrictor choking my neck.

"Daddy. I want a dolphin for Christmas!"

"No." I won't even spend a second entertaining this nonsense. I already have to listen to her constant begging for a puppy, a kitty, a pony, etc. Keeping myself and two children alive is plenty enough for me.

Evangeline shakes with excitement as she's lead out to the middle of our enclosure. Her hand lifts to her mouth, and she blows her sister and me a kiss before tuning in to whatever the guide is telling her. Then she's off. My heart swells with insurmountable pride. There is nothing else in the world like this feeling, knowing I put that huge smile on her face.

"Come on, Daddy," Mary says.

Vangie hasn't yet stopped grinning when she grabs Willow from my arms, pushing me out into the water.

Mary repeats her instructions then steps back. Before I've even stretched my arms all the way out, I feel something hard nudge my ass. *What the f—?* My body jerks, and I reach behind me, blindly swatting as I try to figure out what's just assaulted me.

"No, Christian!" Mary shouts, making some gesture to the huge mammal that's probably about to eat me, just before his snout is back between my legs.

"Daddy!" Willow screams. "Help my daddy!"

Trying not to panic, I kick my legs at the beast. "Get!"

"I'm so sorry, sir. It's breeding season," Mary shrugs, trying not to laugh with the rest of our crew when the horny dolphin continues poking around between my legs like a dog.

"Ew!" Evangeline shouts. "Daddy, his thing is sticking out! Oh my God. He wants to have sex with you!"

Sex? Did my baby just say the words *thing* and *sex*? Then what she said registers, and I push that problem aside for another day because I'm about to get raped by a fucking dolphin.

"Sir, calm down. I'm going to try to get him off of you," Mary gets out between guffaws.

"I'm not about to just float here and let him have his way with me." My feet are now frantically kicking at the randy, four-hundred pound defiler. I don't stand a fucking chance. He's twice my size.

"Daddy," Willow cries. "Watch out! It has a snake tummin' outta its tail. It's gunna bite you!"

I make the mistake of looking and damn near pass out. His fucking dick is as big as my arm. My heart is about to explode with how rapidly it's beating. I can't fucking breathe. I think I may be hyperventilating.

The next thing I know there are a few other trainers in the water trying to persuade the rapist dolphin to leave me alone, and my girls are nowhere to be seen. "Where are my kids?"

"We had everyone else leave the tank as a safety precaution."

At least I know neither of my girls will be Christian's next victim.

"Gigi!" Willow shouts just as we're finally making it out to the beach area to relax and unwind from my attack before heading back onto the cruise ship. My heart dips as I spin around looking to see if that damn woman is actually here. *They weren't supposed to be here*, I whine in my subconscious. Sure enough, my daughter is already cuddled up in her lap beneath a thatched hut near the water.

"Landon! I didn't think I'd get to see you today." Evangeline runs into that boy's waiting arms, and I have the sudden urge to hurl.

This vacation is the dumbest idea I've ever had. Vangie's got a boyfriend, I twisted my ankle, my dick got puked on, and I was sexually harassed by a fucking dolphin.

"Thought you were swimming with dolphins today?" Landon returns, kissing the side of her face. He has the good sense to blush when I shoot him a pair of warning eyes.

Motherfucker.

I purse my lips at Vangie, warning her not to talk about it. But Willow takes it upon herself to be my life ruiner. And to think, she used to be my favorite. "We swam with dolphins, and a snake crawled outta one's butt and it was chasing Daddy. He almost died!"

"What!?" Savage shouts, looking up from the sand fort he's been so busily working on. "That is so cool. I wish I coulda saw."

Confusion mars Gina's face. "Wait...what?"

"It got a hard-on when it was Dad's turn to ride." Vangie blushes. "I thought it was going to drown him." My daughter and I are going to have a good long talk about her vocabulary soon. Is she old enough to know about hard-ons? I don't want her to be.

Tink's lips pull in, flattening into a straight line, then her cheeks hollow out as she tries extra hard to hold her laughter.

"Oh, go on," I grumble, falling into the empty lounge chair beside her. All of the other huts are taken. I decide I'll endure her company just for a place to rest. Fighting off Christian's cock was exhausting.

As soon as she has my blessing, she folds over in hysterics. Spit sprays from her mouth. "How—how big was it?" she finally asks once she gets ahold of herself.

The kids have run off, out of hearing distance to splash in the water, so I humor her. "Like two feet." I inwardly cringe visualizing it.

"No shit..." I can see the wheels in her head turning. "That's impressive."

"I can honestly say that I wasn't all that impressed."

"Did you get any pictures?" she asks.

Shaking my head, I stare at the beautiful vixen beside me. "I wasn't exactly worried about snapping pictures of my assailant's weapon. Sorry."

"S'okay...I just have a fascination with penises."

"Is that so?" I ask, although this doesn't surprise me in the least.

Gina nods, cracking a big grin. "Like, did you know sea slugs lose their dicks every time they have sex? It stays hard and just drags the ground 'til it falls off."

"Kind of like a bee loses its stinger?"

"Not exactly. They don't die...It just breaks off and floats away...Then they grow a new one within a day and are ready to do it all over again."

Automatically my thoughts drift to what happens to that penis once it starts to float off into the ocean, and I shiver.

"What?"

"I was just thinking of the poor unsuspecting fish that's gonna eat that rogue pecker, thinking it's a worm."

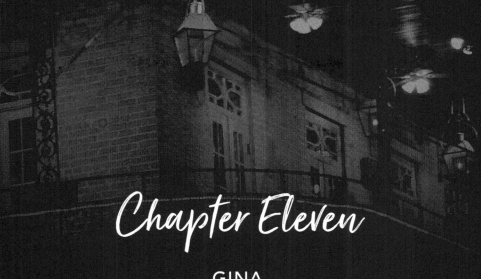

Chapter Eleven

GINA

"Hey, Spence," I answer, rubbing crusties from my eyes. It's still pitch black in our room, but that doesn't mean a thing. Our cabin is in the center of the ship, with no windows. If not for my alarm clock and godsons ensuring I get out of bed each day, I'd probably sleep the whole week away.

"Gi...Don't tell me you were still asleep. It's after nine. Don't y'all have ziplining today?"

Yawn. "Yep. I was just about to get up and wake the kids. We meet at the port at half past ten."

"You sound like you had a late night?" Spence teases.

Did I ever. After my pussy took a pounding riding fucking horses in Belize yesterday, Jeff beat it to a pulp when he nailed me behind a row of stacked chairs once the main deck cleared out last night. I don't know how the hell I'll handle the harness between my legs today. "Yeah, Jeff and I hung out in the comedy club then met back up and uh..." I shine my phone toward the bunks to see if the kids are still sleeping, "hooked up," I whisper, "after we got the kids to sleep."

My best friend clears her throat loudly. "You and Jeff sure have been doing a lot of *hooking up* on this trip."

"Stop," I hiss. "It's convenient. And he has the biggest penis I've ever seen."

"You sure this isn't more than sex?"

No. "Yes," I lie. "I told you...Landon is seeing his older daughter, and the other is trying to trap Savage into marriage. We're together most of the time, and I like his penis...a lot."

"I miss Coop's penis," my best friend whines into the phone.

"Quit," I growl. "What did I tell you about talking to me about his dick? We're like siblings. It's fucking weird, Spencer."

"But you love talking about penises."

"Not his!"

"But bestie, you're the only person I can complain to." Oh man, here come the horny tears. "I still have five more weeks of no sex, which means it will be at least three before I can convince him to fuck me. I'm dying."

"Oh damn, look at the time...I gotta get these kids up and ready to go."

"You're a terrible friend."

I glance back over to the sleeping pile of *her* children and roll my eyes. "The worst. Now go make out with your husband or something while I take *your* children to have some fun."

A loud sob nearly pierces my eardrum, and I yank the phone away. "Oh, God. I'm sorry, Gigi. You're the best friend in the whole world. I didn't even mean that."

"I know. I'm used to you and your post-baby, orgasm-deprived ass by now. No worries."

"I love you, Gina."

"Love you too, bestie." After smooching my lips at her a

few times I end the call, then round up my troops and head out to meet the Ryans, who happen to be on the same excursion as us today.

"Hello, everyone! My name is Rafiki, and I am going to make sure you have the time of your lives here at Family Zipline Tours of Roatan. You did the right thing booking your excursion with us." His Jamaican-style accent and box braids make me smile. It feels so Caribbean. "Children under five years will go over there." Rafiki points to a kid-sized obstacle course with zip lines that can't be but four to five feet from the ground. "We have lots of island mamas to watch over your little ones and ensure they have a safe and fun time."

Savage of course groans, loudly. "Ugh. Why can't I come on the big ones with you? I'm not a baby."

"You'll be big enough next time. It's a good thing you met Willow though. You'll have a friend to play with." I try to sound encouraging, but all he does is roll his eyes.

"Yeah, husban, you getta pway wif me." Willow takes Kyle by the arm and begins pulling him toward the group of women who've just arrived to fetch them.

"Kyle?" Jeff calls and the two little ones spin back around. "Will you look out for Willow for me? You're very mature for your age, and she doesn't like being around strangers."

Kyle's face brightens considerably, and he nods, giving the CEO a thumbs up.

"Thank you for that," I say watching my little man puff up his chest and walk over to join the guides with his pride back intact.

"It was nothing," Jeff says, shrugging me off. "He just needed his big-boyhood stroked a little."

"What about you?" I ask, snickering.

"What about me?" Jeff leans in close, his breath hot against my ear. I can smell the cinnamon in his Big Red gum. I want to grab his face and eat it, but the kids are around, and that would be horribly inappropriate.

"Do you need your *big*-boyhood stroked as well?"

"Eww, Aunt Gina!" Lake shouts, causing every head in our group to turn in my direction. Guess that didn't come out as quiet as I thought.

Jeff's body vibrates next to mine with the force of his laughter as I tuck my head into his shoulder.

"Can I help you with something?" Rafiki pauses his safety speech to ask.

"No, sir. Sorry. Gina here has really bad gas and just let one rip. You know teen boys." Jeff shrugs pointing with his thumb to Lake and Landon and everyone giggles.

"Great!" I grumble. "Thanks for that. Now I'll be known as *fart girl* the whole trip."

"Are you sure this thing won't drop me?" I ask the guide as he straps my harness to the zippy thingie. I'm the last in our crew, and in hindsight, I probably should have gone first, because watching them all fly over the jungle has done nothing to settle my nerves. In fact, it may have made it worse. I could be having a heart attack. "Is it normal for my heart to beat this fast?" I ask the man, who's getting a kick out of my fear.

"Ma'am, you just watched your children and husband do it.

You will be fine."

My wha? "He's not my husbaaaa—" My stomach plummets to my toes as I'm sent flying a hundred feet over a ravine. The rush of the wind is smothering me. I can't freaking breathe. Oh God. No. No, no, no. A sudden and extreme urge to urinate has me twisting my ankles together. *Will this fucking thing ever reach the other end?*

"Oh my God," Lake yells when I'm about halfway across the line. "Did she just pee? Guys, I think she peed!"

Warm urine trickles down my crossed legs, saturating my socks and the insides of my shoes. As if that isn't bad enough, I'm so shocked that I let go of the fucking rope and flip upside down. I'm now dangling in a harness by my beat-up, traitorous pussy, the remaining drops of pee working down my body with the force of gravity, splashing on my lip. I'm screaming and flailing, which is probably not the best course of action. Closing my eyes, I try to keep perfectly still so I don't wiggle my way out of the harness that right now is literally my lifeline.

When I finally make it all the way across, there are tears streaming down my face, or hell, it could even be pee. At this point, who knows? This is truly the most frightening experience of my life, and all of these motherfuckers are laughing. "What the hell is wrong with y'all?" I shout. "I could have died! What if I'd slipped out of that harness? Huh? Would it be so funny then?"

The tour guide at the landing helps me back upright and unclips me from the zipper. "I'm never doing that shit again," I announce, pushing past the guys.

"I have an extra change of clothes in my bag...if you'd like to change," Evangeline offers.

"I love you, sweet child. I would kiss you, but my lips are

full of piss. Got any wipes in that fanny pack of yours?"

"Well, at least one good thing will come of this," Jeff announces.

"What's that?" I ask, grabbing a handful of wipes to clean my face.

He worries his bottom lip between his teeth, mulling over whether or not he should say whatever smartass thing is running through that head of his. Of course, he makes the wrong decision. "I think it's safe to say you no longer have to worry about being known as fart girl."

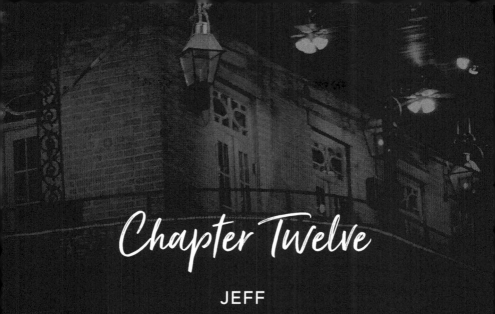

Chapter Twelve

JEFF

"All right you two, knock it off." I glare at Evangeline and Landon with their tongues practically down each other's throats. What the hell happened to no kissing? No one listens to me anymore. "Come on, Vangie, it's time to go."

"I can't believe it's over, Daddy," she sobs. "This has been the best week of my life. I'm never going to see him again." Is this the same kid who just seven days ago thought having to go on this trip was the worst thing to ever happen to her?

"You'll live," I grumble. "Take care, boys...Gina." I wave and pull my crying girls over to the customs counter so we can be on our way.

The ride home is pure misery. Evangeline has somehow decided it's my fault that the week has come to an end and is shooting me daggers from the passenger side of my truck. Willow is crying for her Gigi and Tyle, and for some reason unbeknownst to me, there's a hollow feeling in my gut that just grows larger the farther we drive away.

"Well, this is depressing," I grumble as I turn into the driveway of our house. Evangeline is still crying into her hands. Willow has managed to cry herself to sleep, but every few seconds lets out a sniffle.

"You don't even care!" she shouts, throwing the door open. "I'm going to Savana's."

"That's fine, but you owe me a clean room before you leave. Remember? Best daddy everrrrr!" I tease, trying to cheer her up.

Apparently, I know less than nothing about teenaged girls, because my attempt at humor only seems to further irritate her.

"I wish Mom was still alive," she wails, jumping out of my truck and slamming the door.

I climb out after her, intercepting my daughter in the driveway before she runs inside to lock herself in her room. "That was a joke, Evangeline. I never expected you to actually clean your room."

She sniffles, and I can feel her body tremble from where I'm holding her arm. "I really like him, Daddy." What's left of my heart shrivels up. My little girl has an honest-to-God broken heart, and I'm making fun of her over it.

Goddamn it. These girls need their mother. I don't have what it takes to raise females. I'm going to screw them up so bad. "I'm sorry, princess." I pull her in for a hug, kissing the top of her head. "I wasn't trying to hurt you."

"You think, maybe one day we can meet up for lunch or at a park or something?" she asks. My baby looks so hopeful that I can't crush her with the truth, that we just live too far apart.

"I'm sure we can work something out eventually, honey."

"Thanks, Daddy," she says, throwing her arms around my neck.

"Sure thing. Go on inside and unpack and make sure it's

okay with Savana's mom for you to come over. I'm gonna go get Willow out of the truck."

"How was the trip?" My brother and business partner Victor asks, after we get Willow and his six-year-old son, Maddox to bed. He only has Maddox every other weekend—the product of a one-night stand. Often times they end up crashing at my place instead of his bachelor pad.

I scrub a hand over my face, leaning back in my recliner, and sigh. What a loaded question. "It was...interesting, to say the least. The girls ended up having a good time though, so that's all that matters."

"Let me guess? You stayed in the room the whole time wallowing in your misery. Dude...I can't believe you went on a cruise with free babysitting and didn't get trashed and fool around a little. Everyone knows singles go there to hook up."

My God, he makes my head hurt. "I took my girls on a family vacation, Victor. It wasn't about me."

"It's *never* about you, Jeff."

Yeah, well. It's *always* about him. I don't say what I'm thinking, though. I'm not in the mood for a fight tonight. Instead, I proceed to fill him in on my series of unfortunate events, ending with the rapist dolphin.

My brother cracks up. "They say dolphins are sensitive creatures. He could probably sense how badly you needed to get laid. Even the fucking fish felt sorry for you, bruh."

For some reason I choose to keep what happened with Tink and me to myself. It's not like I'll ever see her again, but I don't want to cheapen what happened between us by bragging about it to this numbskull. Huh. Guess somewhere along the way she grew on me a little.

"Jeff. Yoohoo, Jeff," my brother calls, snapping his fingers in front of my face.

"Yeah?"

"Where were you, man?"

I shake my head, bringing myself back to the present. "Just spaced for a sec. What's up?"

"Why don't you call that chick? The one you've been fucking...Go over to her place and bang one out? I got these kids under control."

I can't help but to laugh. "I bet you do...they're passed out."

He shrugs. "Then you know you can trust me." He tips his hat like he's doing me some great service then takes a long pull from his beer. "Don't say I never did anything for ya."

The thought of hooking up with anyone else right now makes me physically ill. It's probably just because I've had more sex in the last week than the past three years. "I'm good, Vic. I'm really not in the mood."

His mouth falls open in mock shock. "Not in the mood for fucking? How do we share the same DNA, little brother?"

Chapter Thirteen

GINA

"Well, if it ain't Miss Pissypants herself," Coop says, grabbing Kyle's luggage from my hands and kissing my cheek.

"You told him!" I accuse, glaring at my best friend over his shoulder.

"She tells me everything." His face crinkles up, and he shrugs his shoulders.

"Not *everything*," Spence counters, walking up with her arms open wide for her little demon spawn. "My babies! I missed you so much. Did you have fun? Did Gina behave?"

What the—? "Um, aren't you supposed to ask me if they behaved?"

"One would think," Mrs. Elaine chimes, entering the room with one of the girls in her arms.

"Now don't you start in on me too, old woman," I warn my best friend's mom, who is more of a mother to me than my own, as I walk over and kiss her cheek. Then I snatch the pretty little bundle from her arms. "Which one is this?" I ask, kissing her little forehead. My Lord, she smells good enough to eat. My insides turn all warm and gooey.

"Stop sniffing her," Coop's mom Nelly orders. "You might've picked up some germs on that ship."

"Damn, you're here too? What is this? A party? Is there booze?" I ask, trying to rile Cooper's mother. "I could go for a margarita!"

"No drunk baby holding." Nelly walks over and tries to pry my goddaughter from my arms, but I spin around like a ninja because I'll be damned if she's gonna stop me from finally getting the chance to love up on these babies.

"You sound like Jeffrey. I wasn't *really* going to drink anything. Let me get my baby fix." I walk away from the baby hog, hiding behind Spencer for protection.

"That's Abigail," my bestie says. "We've been dressing her in pink and Emmaline in yellow, 'til everyone can tell them apart."

"That's really smart."

She nods. "Oh, and don't think I didn't catch that Jeffrey comment. Just fucking, my ass."

"Wait!" Coop says, rising from where he's crouched on the floor with Savage. "Is that...Can we? I hadn't even thought of the back door."

Spencer's head whips around. "And you can just unthink it right now, mister."

"Hasn't anyone ever told you that marriage is about sacrifice?"

"It's really not that bad, Spence," I encourage, not even trying to hide my laughter. "You'll only bleed the first few times."

"Y'all need Jesus," Nelly says, ushering the boys out of the room and away from our entirely inappropriate conversation. I hear her muttering about what a bad influence I am, and how these children would likely be better off raised by wolves than the lot of us. But I don't think we're doing so bad. They're the coolest little assholes I know.

"Yeah, I'm bleeding enough, thankyouverymuch," my best friend says, heading for the living room.

"How're your diaper changing skills now, Daddy-oh?" I ask Cooper as we trail behind Spencer to the living room. "You a pro yet?"

"Well, I haven't sprayed either of them down with the hose, so that's progress, right?"

A few years ago, he decided to break Savage out of daycare, and during his foray into babysitting, he experienced his first shit explosion diaper. It ended with the bed of his truck covered in poop, and Kyle soaked head to toe.

"Baby steps."

"I've only puked twice," he adds, all proud of himself.

"AND THERE WAS THIS DOLPHIN that had a snake swimming out of its butt. It almost ate Willow's daddy!" Kyle gushes between bites of spaghetti.

"It wasn't a snake," Lake clarifies to all of the stupefied faces around the table. "It was his penis, and he was trying to mount Mr. Jeffrey."

Mrs. Elaine crosses herself, mumbling a string of curses beneath her breath. The sign of the cross and a string of profanities… that about sums this woman up perfectly, God love her.

"Nuh-unh," Kyle argues, slamming his little fist down on the table. "Willow said it was a snake, right, Auntie?" His little puppy dog eyes look to me for confirmation. Heat floods my cheeks as I debate the safest way to answer this.

"That is exactly what Willow said."

Chapter Fourteen

GINA

"I can't believe I let you two talk me into this," I grumble, glaring at Mom and Dad, who are both eyeing me through the rearview mirror as we pull up behind a freaking Bentley at Uncle Ricky and Aunt Martha's Victorian mansion. Ever since I was a little girl, I dreamed of someday living in a house like this in the Garden District: the ornate architecture and huge white columns, balconies and courtyards filled with the most beautiful gardens. The homes are like something straight from a fairytale. And even though I know I'll never have the husband and children to make a house like this a home, I still wanted it. And I have Dillon Bourque to thank for snatching the rug right out from under my feet.

"You and Dillon were so close, honey. It's been over two years. You need to get over it."

"Get over it?" I growl. "That asshole ruined my career, Mom! He humiliated me...And not just me, but Spencer too. He didn't even think about the two of us or what it would do to her *children* when he decided to—"

"Gina," my father deadpans. "When that boy was screwing Clarissa Dubois, I guarantee you and Spencer were the last people on his mind. No offense."

The proud grin on my father's face has my blood boiling. Dillon never could do any wrong in his eyes. "It's not funny, Dad. She was our client. What he did was not okay. He fucked her in our office!"

"Oh, come now, Gina. It's a little funny." I don't think my mother has ever had an authentic thought, always echoing Dad's opinions.

"Ugh," I huff, climbing out of the back seat of my mother's Camry. "He got the clinic shut down and destroyed my reputation. Excuse me if I don't see the humor in that." I will never forgive him. NOLA Sexual Health was my future. I had a job that I loved right in the heart of New Orleans. Thanks to his inability to keep his dick in his trousers, I lost it all.

"Fix your face," Mom orders, rushing to my side. She looks ridiculous in her mermaid string bikini. I swear the woman lives to embarrass me. I just know she and Dad will be making out like fucking teenagers once they get a few drinks in. "Ricky is your father's brother, and he and Martha adore you." Her hand grips mine, halting my stride. "They're so excited that you've decided to join us today. Don't ruin it for them."

"You have to let this go, Gina. You can't continue to blame the man for doing what men do."

My father is such a pig. "Daddy," I say, yanking my wrist from my mother's hold. "Don't...Just don't come at me with your chauvinistic crap today because I will Uber my ass right back home to Cedar Grove."

"You're awful—ummm—bitchy," my mother whispers the last word. "Maybe Dillon could hook you up with one of his friends?" She smiles wide, her green eyes shining with mirth. "Just like old times." Mom's brows do a little bounce as she and my father both crack up laughing.

I can't even count how many times I got busted fooling around with my older cousin's friends. We really were a mess growing up. And to be honest, I do miss him. But I just may hate him more. Guess I'll know the answer to that in a few minutes.

"Ginaaa!" my Aunt Martha squeals, shuffling out of the house to greet me. She wraps her toned arms around my chest, nearly squeezing the breath from my lungs.

"Hey, Aunt Martha." I hug her back, and tears spring to my eyes. I didn't realize just how much I missed her. Out of sight, out of mind, I guess. She smells of cookies and cakes. Martha is your classic fifties housewife. Her long blonde hair is in a perfect updo, her navy shift dress starched to perfection. I swear I've never seen the woman not put together. "Still baking?"

"You know it! I made a batch of your favorite cookies and hid a few from these vultures. Had to make sure my princess got hers." She steps back, sliding her hands down my arms until she's holding me by the fingers. Aunt Martha doesn't even attempt to hide the tears spilling down her cheeks. "I missed you so much, child."

"Me, too." God, I feel like shit for not coming around to visit her. It's not her fault her son's a whore.

"He misses you too, you know," she adds, sniffling.

A lump forms in my throat, and I swallow that bitch down, forcing a smile and a nod. I know he does. He's called and left more messages than I can count. I'm just as stubborn as they come.

"Well, come on." My aunt drops my hands and begins

moving toward the door.

When I step into the foyer, I'm hit with a sense of nostalgia. I spent a few weeks of every summer in this house growing up. No matter how awful I was—and trust me I was a hot mess— I was always welcomed back with open arms.

"Gigi!" Uncle Ricky croons intercepting me on my trek to the kitchen. "So nice of you to grace us with your presence."

"Missed you too, Uncle Ricky." He lifts me clean off the ground, enveloping me in his big, burly arms, just like he used to when we were kids. My uncle is a mammoth of a man, standing six foot four. I don't think I've ever seen him clean shaven and always loved to tease that I could braid the hair on his arms. He's truly intimidating to look at, but I've never known a kinder soul. Uncle Ricky is a big, old teddy bear.

"Put me down," I squeal as he throws me over his shoulder and carries me through the house, out the French doors, straight to the backyard. My ass feels so exposed, sticking up in the air like this. As I wriggle around in his arms, trying to tug my short pink dress to cover my exposed bathing suit bottom, we finally reach the pool, and he sets me on my feet right in front of that arrogant bastard Dillon.

"I hate you," I whisper beneath my breath to Uncle Ricky, who's got a shit grin from ear to fucking ear.

"Love you too, pumpkin." He plants a kiss on the top of my head before announcing my presence. "Hey guys," he says to the group of middle-aged men who were just deep in conversation with he who has been my sworn enemy for the last few years. "Most of you remember our little Gigi, right?"

A couple of heads bob, and I vaguely hear a few greetings. My attention is singularly focused on Mr. GQ himself, with his stupid muscles and too-pretty hair. If he weren't so damned attractive none of this would have happened, and we could still be best friends.

Dillon's bright blue eyes widen, as if he's staring at a ghost. "Gina?"

"I haven't changed that damn much," I snark, trying to hide the overwhelming wave of emotion behind my signature sass.

He shakes his head with a laugh. "You haven't changed a bit," he agrees, setting his Bud Light on the table and scrubbing a hand over his face. "I'm sorry," he whispers, staring me right in the eyes. "I'm so fucking sorry."

Goddamn it. I'm not going to fucking cry in front of all these people. *Deep breaths, Gina.* Just as I'm about to cave, I spot a familiar face sitting across the wrought iron table from Dillon. An ex-client—none other than Clarissa Dubois. "What the hell is she doing here?"

I ignore the little tramp's indignant squeal and the snorts of laughter and gasps from our audience, pleading with all that is holy that there is some explanation, apart from the obvious, for her presence at our *family* Fourth of July gathering.

Dillon coughs. "Uh, I didn't realize you'd be here, Gigi."

"Why. Is. She. Here?"

"We're together," he mutters. It comes out all jumbled like one long curse, but there is no mistaking what he's just said.

"I'm sorry...You're to—what?" He's got to be fucking with me right now. "You were supposed to be helping fix their sex life, not stealing his wife, Dillon!"

"Can we talk about this in private?" Dillon begs, glancing around at all of our family's shocked faces. "They don't—well *didn't*—know."

"Yeah, thanks, Gina," Clarissa chimes in. "Now they'll all think I'm a ho."

"If the shoe fits, lace that bitch up."

Clarissa looks around, her face growing pinker by the second. "You don't even know me," she grits out.

"I know you had a sweet husband who worshiped the fucking ground you walked on. Who cared enough to try to save your marriage by going to freaking sex therapy. Do you have any idea how hard that is for a man to do? And you thanked him by not only fucking said therapist, but leaving him for the therapist?"

I hear Aunt Martha gasp behind me and turned to apologize. The next thing I know, I'm flat on my back, my head inches from the pool, with my former client wailing away at me. Her sudden attack takes me completely by surprise, but it's not long before our roles are reversed, and I've got two fists full of her weave, ready to yank it out. How dare she attack me like this?

"Tink?" The lone word stops me in my tracks. It can't be...

"Jeffrey?" I answer, costing myself a jab to the cheekbone as I search through the shocked faces gawking at us to find the man I haven't been able to stop thinking about for the last month.

He rushes over, and before I realize what's happening, I'm in his arms, my back to his chest and the skank in Dillon's. My anger forgotten, the only thought in my head is how good it feels to be held by this man again. "You smell like beer," I mutter, and he laughs. The vibration of his laughter against my back has me turning to putty in his familiar arms.

"Your lip's bleeding," he counters, lifting the hand that's across my chest to touch his thumb to my swollen cheek. "You'll have a nice shiner here."

Spinning around in his arms, I touch each of my hands to the sides of his face, relishing the feel of the coarse stubble against my palms. "You don't drink." I can't get past the smell of alcohol on his breath and the overwhelming desire I have to taste it on his tongue. My heart is racing. It's as if everyone else has just disappeared, and Jeffrey and I are the only two people in existence.

Jeffrey's head shakes. "I said I don't drink around my kids."

Ah. His kids aren't here—wait...why is *he* here? "Wh—what are you doing here?"

Jeff pushes my hair behind my ears; his fingers never stop touching me as he speaks. "The girls are with Jessica's mother for the weekend. So, I went out last night...and ran into an old buddy from college. He invited me over and here I am."

"Dillon."

Jeff clears his throat. "Yeah, he an ex of yours or something? What the hell was that?"

"That," I answer, trailing my eyes back over to Dillon and Clarissa, "is the reason I had to leave New Orleans."

Chapter Fifteen

JEFFREY

"Thought you didn't catch feelings?" There's a bite to my tone, and I'm feeling something a little too reminiscent of jealousy for my liking. But I'll be damned if it doesn't piss me off to imagine his hands on Tink. To see her scrapping it out with another woman over a man who isn't me. Not that I want her feeling possessive over me. I don't. Right? Of course not.

A knowing smile curls her lips. "Would it bother you, Jeffrey?" She smooths her hands over the front of my chest, and when her fingertip brushes my nipple, my dick begins to harden. I'm positive that I've never wanted to fuck so badly. Ever.

"No," I lie. "I just need to know what I'm up against here, Tink."

"Meaning?"

"That was a hell of a show for someone who doesn't get attached."

"Dude, chill," Dillon interrupts, reminding me that there

are people standing around, listening in on our conversation. "We're cousins. Trust me, if there's one girl who won't lose her head over a guy, it's that heartless bitch."

"I can speak for myself, asshole." Gina's ready to duke it out with Dillon now. She's like a little Chihuahua.

"All right, Ronda Rousey, that's enough," I tease, taking us both by surprise when I silence her with my mouth. Cheers erupt around us, but I couldn't care less. Her lips are soft, and pliant. Her tongue desperate and seeking. And her nails feel so good digging into my shoulders.

"You taste so good," she murmurs into my mouth, causing me to chuckle.

"Such a fucking alcoholic." I pull back and run my thumb along her lower lip.

"I take it you two know each other?" Dillon asks.

"We fucked a few times on the ship last month," Gina announces. To her whole family. Just like she'd be announcing that she saw a movie last week.

Her dad cracks a huge smile, and I want the ground to split open and swallow me up. What a fucking weirdo.

"Gina!" Martha gasps. "Honey, I wish you wouldn't treat sex like a...a *man*. You deserve someone who'll worship and adore you."

"Stop." Gina gives her aunt a no-nonsense look. "Don't you dare slut-shame me."

"I'm not. I ju—"

"Come with me?" Gina says, dismissing her aunt. She grabs my hand, and I follow her through the crowd, back into the house. She leads me down a long dark hall before finally opening a door and ushering me inside.

"The laundry room?"

"Jeffrey, I need you to fuck me." This woman never ceases to shock me with the things that come out of her mouth.

"What?" I look around at the confined space. "In here?"

She nods her head as she saunters toward me. "Right here, CEO. Right now." Tink's hand goes straight to the bulge in my khaki shorts, and she begins kneading my dick. "If you're not up to it, I'm sure I could go out there and find another friend of my cousin's who'd be more than willing to help me blow off some steam."

I grip her hair in my fist and tug until her eyes lock with mine. "I'm more than up to it."

"Good," she says, backing up to the dryer. Her hands creep up her thighs slowly, lifting the skirt of her pink sundress. When her thumbs hook into the band of her bikini bottom, I can hardly breathe with how badly I want to be inside of this woman again. I can't take my eyes off her as she does a little shimmy, sliding them down the length of her legs and flicking it across the room. "I'm dripping, Jeffrey."

Holy shit. "Yeah?" Advancing on her, I grip the backs of Tink's thighs, hoisting her up onto the top of the vibrating dryer.

"Grab a sock from that basket over there and tie it to the outside of the doorknob." Gina points to an unmatched mountain of socks hidden away in the corner of the room.

"Are we suddenly back in college?"

Her eyes roll. "Jeffrey, this is a utility room. There's no lock. Do you want someone to just walk in on us?"

"A sock? Really?"

"Everyone knows what a sock on the door means, CEO. And my family is very aware of who I am as a person. Trust me. They know exactly what we're doing back here. When they see the sock, it will instantly click."

"I don't know how I feel about having sex with you in the same house as your parents...and them knowing." I'd have *never* talked about having sex so casually with my mom and dad, much less Jessica's.

"Drying up like the fucking Sahara over here, Jeff. You're killing my buzz."

"Just so you know," I say, as I grab a damn sock and quickly knot it around the knob. "I'm leaving as soon as we finish."

"I'd expect nothing more from you, Jeffrey."

"I mean it. I'm not sticking around to deal with the awkward aftermath."

"It's fine. I just want you for your cock." She winks then slips the dress over her head, leaving her in a white bikini top and nothing else.

There's a brief moment where I worry about the possibility of humiliating myself with a case of whiskey dick. I don't drink often now that it's just me and my girls. But one look at this beautiful blonde trussed up on that machine with her legs parted, dipping her fingers inside and swirling her own juices around her clit, has me about to come in my shorts. "You're so fucking sexy, Tink," I groan as I retrieve a condom from my wallet, drop my pants, and roll it on.

She's moaning before I've even touched her. No girl has ever performed for me this way. Oh, who am I kidding? This isn't for my benefit at all. Tink is lost in her own world. Chasing her release. Hell, I'm not even sure she remembers I'm in the room until she starts moaning my name.

"Keep going, babe," I encourage, placing my hands on the top of the dryer and bringing my mouth to her pussy. I drive my tongue in and out while she moans and writhes against my face. When I feel her body tensing up and I know that she's close, I grip her thighs and pull her to the edge, slamming into her in one quick thrust.

"Jeffrey!" she screams. "Oh, God, I love your cock." Her legs wrap around my waist, and as she rides my dick, she goes on about how massive it is and how she's been up at night craving it. I really wish I could let her continue because my ego is thoroughly enjoying this, but she's going to get us busted.

"Shhh," I whisper, taking her mouth with mine as I rock in and out of her tight, warm, channel. The vibration heightens every sensation. We're both seconds away from exploding together when the door creaks open.

Gina and I both freeze. I'm sure neither of us is even breathing when a hand holding a dirty towel appears through the opening. Tink's nails dig into my ass cheeks when the door moves another fraction of an inch.

"Who put a damn sock on the door?" Martha shouts.

Shit. Fuck. We are so busted.

"Oh my God, Mom! Shut the damn door." There's a slight scuffle, and then the door slams and I can hear Dillon explaining the sock to his clueless mother as they move down the hall and away from the laundry room.

Chapter Sixteen

GINA

"Wait! Where are you going?" As soon as the door closed, the CEO withdrew his glorious erection and began stuffing it back into his clothes. "I wasn't finished."

He gives me an "are you fucking kidding me" look, to which I lift my brows in an unspoken, "does it look like I'm kidding?" stare in return.

"Gina, I can't. I'm sorry. I have to get the fuck outta here. This is too weird for me."

Horny tears well up in my eyes. "Please don't do this to me." Goddamn it. Why do I sound so weak and needy? It's just a dick, Gina. You can find another, like that. I snap my fingers for effect in my subconscious. But I don't want another, I argue with myself. I want that one.

Jeff's eyes fall while his lips twist into a smirk. I can't tell if he feels sorry for me or is trying not to laugh. "Tink," he croons, walking over to the dryer and slipping my dress over my head. "Why don't you come with me? Let's go grab a drink."

"Look at you, tempting the lush with booze," I mock pout. "Such a dad move."

At that he bursts out laughing. "Most dads don't try bribing their daughters with alcohol, Tink."

I shrug. "Well, mine would...but I meant you trying to make me all squirrely by dangling a shiny new toy in front of my face."

He bites down on his lower lip, looking at me with puppy dog eyes. "Is it working?"

Sigh. "Maybe. I'd much prefer the toy you have dangling between your legs, though." While running my tongue over my lips, I trail my big toe over his crotch.

"Later," Jeff says, taking my hands into his and pulling me down from the dryer. "I'm having a little performance anxiety." He reaches into his pocket, pulling out my suit bottom and presses it into my hand. "Get dressed."

It's not hard for us to sneak out unnoticed. Everyone is either gathered in the kitchen for food or out back, in and around the pool. After a quick peek down the hall, we walk right through the front door.

"I've always loved this place," I muse aloud, while admiring the cobblestone sidewalks and huge live oaks.

"Yeah?" Jeff asks, placing his hand at my lower back. It's warm and feels *nice*. It's so strange just walking and talking like a normal couple, which we are not.

And never will be, I remind myself.

"Yeah. I always thought I'd end up here someday, living in my princess castle with the man of my dreams, 2.5 kids, and a fluffy little white dog."

There's a softness in his features when he responds, "You could still have all of that, Gina."

Forcing myself to smile, I swallow the lump that's just formed in my throat. "Nah. It isn't in the cards for me. But it's really neat to come back and revisit my little girl dreams, you know?"

"Yeah," he answers, taking on a faraway look.

"Shit. It's getting a little too deep for me, CEO. Take me to the booze!"

His head shakes and he huffs out a laugh. "I thought you liked it deep?"

Oh, the old man's got jokes.

We catch the St. Charles trolley, getting off at Canal. I let Jeffrey lead the way, curious to see where we end up.

"A Court of Two Sisters?"

"Best brunch in the city," he answers. "Did you want to go someplace else?"

"No. Their mimosas are great." I don't tell him that this seems a little too date-ish for two people who are just fucking. This is such foreign territory for me. I don't date. I'm not used to being out with a guy unless it's with a group of friends. I'm breaking all of my rules for this man, and I have a sinking feeling that if I'm not careful my heart may get caught up in the crossfire.

We're seated outside in the famous courtyard, right near the huge fountain. "Did you know they call that the Devil's Wishing Well?" I ask the CEO when he returns with his plate overflowing with jambalaya, breakfast potatoes, and eggs.

"I did not. Why do they call it that?" Jeff mumbles through a mouth full of food.

"Ever heard of Marie Laveau?"

"Famous voodoo queen, right?"

I nod. "Well, legend has it that she used to practice in this courtyard and that well," I say, pointing to the fountain with my thumb over my shoulder, "is named in her honor."

"No shit?" He shovels another bite of sausage into his mouth. "That's fascinating, Tink. Ever had your cards read?"

"Uh, no. I have no desire to know when I'm gonna die."

Jeffrey cracks up. "You honestly think they'd tell you that? They want you to come back. It's all a gimmick. They're trying to make a believer out of you, not frighten you half to death."

"Have you had yours read?" I counter.

"Well, no. It all seems silly. Though it's not too hard to figure out that they tell you what they need to in order to keep people coming back. I mean, almost everyone I know is all amazed that their card reader was able to tell that they'd lost a loved one...who hasn't. You know?"

He does have a point. "Well, I still have no desire to have someone digging around in my cards."

"Here you go, ma'am," Our server, Gaston, walks up behind me, setting a much-needed mimosa on a little cocktail napkin then reaches back to his tray for Jeffrey's bloody mary. I cringe to myself, never having been able to get on board with drinking vegetables. "And here you are, sir. Vegetable art courtesy of our head bartender, Marty. Sometimes he likes to get fancy."

Sticking out of his drink is a long, curved green bean with an olive attached to either side, impaled by a toothpick to hold the sculpture together. "It's a dick!" I shout, unable to stop myself from reaching out and touching it.

"Did you just flick my—" Jeff looks at me incredulously.

"Totally just flicked your bean, CEO."

He sucks in his lips, shaking his head. "Just keep your mouth away from that shaft. I have plans to drink this thing."

My cheeks flame. "I was seasick."

My date eyes me skeptically.

"I'll have you know my gag reflex is nonexistent, mister. I'm a professional."

"I'll take your word for it."

"The fucking boat shifted, and your dick was practically in my stomach. I need a chance to redeem myself."

"Yeah," he says with an exaggerated dry heave, "not interested."

By the time I've finished stuffing myself on the best primavera pasta and apple cobbler I've ever eaten, and sucking down a few cocktails, I'm ready for bed. It's not even two in the afternoon.

"Mmm," Jeff moans over a forkful of salad. "Have you tried the balsamic?" he asks after chewing and swallowing. "It's so good."

"It's literally vinegar, Jeff. How good can it be?" And where the hell does he put all this food? He's got to be on his fourth plate by now.

After the waiter finally brings our check, we make our way out into the bustling streets.

"Where to now, boss man?"

"Lady's choice."

All of the dirty places I could take this uptight daddy start rolling through my head. "You sure you wanna hand the reins over to me?"

"Do your worst," he says, gripping my chin in his forefinger and thumb and placing a chaste kiss on the tip of my nose.

My body goes haywire. How can a simple touch stir up such a frenzy? This is the moment I realize that I'm in big, big trouble with this guy.

Chapter Seventeen

JEFFREY

"How'd I know you were gonna take me to a strip club?"

She shrugs her creamy white shoulders. "Must be finally figuring out how awesome I am." Tink grabs my arm, pulling me toward the door to the Hustler Club. "Come on, stiffy. Let's go see some titty-tons."

After paying our covers and the additional fees for VIP, I follow Gina inside. The first thing I notice is how much nicer this place is than any strip club I've ever been to with the guys. Not that I've been to very many—just for a couple of my buddies' bachelor parties. It's not really my thing. Or, it wasn't. While I enjoy a nice pair of tits as much as the next guy, it was always a little uncomfortable knowing Jess was back home stressing over the fact that I was there. Not that I could blame her. I certainly wouldn't have been okay if she were the one out on the town, watching men take off their clothes.

"I can do that." Tink points to the stripper spinning around the top of the stripper pole, which extends all the way up to the ceiling on the second floor.

"Why does that not surprise me?" I lean in close and still have to shout to be heard over the loud music.

"I was never a stripper, Jeffrey." She drags me over to the railing for a closer look. "It looked like fun, so I took lessons."

"You have too much time on your hands."

"Jealous?"

I take a moment to contemplate what I'm sure was meant to be a rhetorical question, and am surprised to realize in some ways I am. I can't imagine not feeling bogged down by the stress of running my company or being the only full-time parent to my kids. But I also can't even fathom how meaningless my life would be without them. "A little," I finally answer, not wanting to make her feel bad about herself by revealing the truth. She's already let it slip that she's unable to have children. If I were being honest, I'd tell her how empty I would feel without my girls. You'd think I'd enjoy having the chance to go out and hook up, but I'm left feeling so hollow the next morning. It's at those times I miss my wife more than ever—where I mourn the intimacy that goes along with sex when there are feelings involved.

"Come here, I wanna show you something." Tink's eyes widen with excitement as she takes my hand, leading me out to a balcony overlooking Bourbon Street. "*This* is why you get VIP at The Hustler Club."

"So, it has nothing to do with the strippers?"

"Duh, them too, but you can get that downstairs. This is worth the extra cash." Gina grabs two hands full of beads from the bucket next to the balcony door, waving them in the air above her head. "Come on ladies, show me those tittays!"

Dear God, she is insane. She's immature and wild, with a

mouth that would make a sailor blush. *Why can't I seem to get enough of her*, I wonder, taking a pull from my beer.

"Don't watch me, idiot. Watch the street. You're about to see some boobies, CEO!"

"My bad." Shaking myself from a daze, I refocus my attention on the sea of drunken chaos below. People from all walks of life are joined together in the spirit of tits and booze. There's a religious man preaching into a microphone a few feet down about the perils of alcohol. The best part of that situation is he's got his two young children with him. Parenting win. I'm pretty sure bringing your kids to Bourbon Street negates your right to judge.

"Throw me somethin', mister!" a half-naked brunette shouts, lifting her cropped tee. Two large tits pop out. She shimmies, jiggling them from side to side.

An elbow digs into my side. "She's talking to you, Jeffrey. Throw her some damn beads."

Oh, yeah. "I feel like a total creep paying that young girl in plastic beads for exposing herself, Tink."

Gina huffs. Her sigh is loud and drawn out. "You're such a dad. Lighten up. These girls know the currency before popping their tits out. It's all about the experience, Jeff. They are having the time of their lives!"

I harrumph. "Yeah, well, let me find out my girls ever try—"

"Jeffrey," Tink warns, fisting her hand into the front of my shirt. "I adore your kids—I do. But, we're at a strip club...Can you take the dad hat off for a few hours and just be a hot, sexy, single dude out with a very horny sexual goddess for one night? Huh? I *really* need the happy ending promised at the end of this *not date*." Her hands come around my waist and venture into my back pockets, where she gives my ass cheeks a good squeeze.

Gina's right. "Sorry. I'll try not to be such a buzzkill," I breathe the promise into the top of her hair while rattling the Mardi Gras necklaces over the ledge with one hand. The other, I wrap around her back, pressing her body harder against my own. In this alcohol-induced haze, it's easy to ignore the faint warning going off in my mind that's telling me it's time to pull away. I've got enough wits about me to know I'm letting things go too far, but just enough of a buzz not to care. I haven't enjoyed a woman's company this much in years.

Tink orders us each a few shots of Fireball, her choice of poison, and we stay out on the balcony throwing beads 'til the sun begins to set. Hours have gone by in the blink of an eye.

"I have a surprise for you," Gina squeals, as she returns from a trip to the bathroom handing me two mystery shots.

"Do you?" I ask, eyeing her. "Why does this frighten me?"

Giggling, she disappears back through the door. "Come on, CEO! And swallow those," she shouts back at me. "You're gonna need 'em."

The little sprite frolics off to a dark little cubbyhole in the back of the room. My pulse speeds up with nervous excitement. "What are you doing?"

"Have a seat, Jeffrey," she orders, pushing down on my shoulders.

"Are you going to strip for me?" I ask, my hubba-hubba brows waggling.

She winks a seductive eye at me. "Something like that."

Suddenly the woman we watched working the pole a few hours earlier appears. "Hey there, Jeffrey," she croons, placing both of her hands on the arms of my chair. Her huge tits are right under my nose, bouncing in her gold bikini top. Her long wavy brown hair tickles my nose. "I'm Misha. Your girl Gina here tells me you deserve a special treat tonight."

My cock rises like a phoenix from the ashes as she scoots her barely covered pussy onto my lap, reaching back to untie her top.

"Would you like her to join you?"

"Oh, no," Gina insists, backing away slowly. "This is all for him."

"Come here, Tink."

"Nuh-uhn. I paid to watch," she persists.

"Come. Here."

Tink swallows hard. I can see her chest rising and falling rapidly.

"Now."

Slowly the sexy little blonde makes her way over to stand before me. Misha steps back allowing us a semiprivate moment.

"Your dress," I rasp, "Take it off."

She grips the hem of her dress, and shimmies, lifting it over her head. Goddamn it. I've never in my life seen anything more beautiful than this woman standing before me in nothing but a bikini. Even without the beer goggles, I know for a fact she'd still be the most exquisite thing I've ever laid eyes on.

"Sit in his lap," Misha orders, taking Gina by the arms and turning her back to my front.

With little hesitation Tink straddles my knees, reverse cowgirl style, spreading her legs and scooting all the way back. "Like this, Jeffrey?" she asks over her shoulder, grinding her ass into my rock-hard dick.

"Y—yeah."

Then Misha begins to roll her hips to the beat of the music, climbing over Gina. The girls compete in an erotic dance off—

in my lap.

"I'm going to fuck you so hard, tonight, Tink," I growl into her ear, cupping her breasts. Sliding my fingers beneath the fabric, I tweak her hard nipples, and she moans in pleasure. Her head falls back to rest on my shoulder, pushing her tits up into the air. I bring my lips to the curve of her neck and suck the sensitive flesh as she writhes against me.

"That was fun guys," Misha says. Her time must be up. Until she spoke just now, I'd managed to forget she was even here.

Gina slips the dancer a wad of cash, and—I'm assuming—thanks her. I'm so close to nutting I can't focus on much else. I haven't come from dry humping since I was a kid, but I'm so fucking close. What I wouldn't give to be able to throw Gina on the floor and give her a good fucking.

"Feel free to stay here a while longer and finish your man off...Just remember," Misha adds with a mischievous grin, "no sex in the champagne room."

"No sex, my ass," Gina says as soon as Misha is out of earshot.

"I'm sorry?" I say, running my tongue up the curve of her neck. "Did you say you want it in your ass?"

"Maybe later," Gina teases, reaching behind her to unzip my pants and then pulls out my dick. "Wrap it," she orders, pulling her suit to the side and slipping two fingers into her pussy.

Let's just say I'm pretty sure I set the world record for suiting up.

Chapter Eighteen

GINA

After Jeffrey gives me two of the best orgasms of my life, one with his monster cock and another with his skilled fingers, we decide it's time to grab some food to soak up some of the alcohol that, according to him, we've both consumed way too much of. Personally, I could go at least a few more rounds.

"You're actually kinda fun when you're inebriated, CEO," I observe as we make our way down to the French Quarter for beignets at Café Du Monde.

"Thanks, Tink." Jeff reaches for my hand, lacing his fingers in mine. My first instinct is to pull away, but it feels nice. Really nice, actually. "You're not as hard to stomach when the kids aren't around," he slurs, his half-assed attempt at a compliment, and I nearly piss myself laughing.

"Wow. You really know how to make a girl feel good, lemme tell ya."

He looks over at me with a wide, goofy grin. "I've always

"Oh my God." He is too much. "I was talking about your Shakespearian way with words."

His face beams with pride. "I'm very charming as well."

Someone has definitely been lying to him. "Uh-huh," I mumble. He's lucky I'm looking forward to him making me feel good for a third time tonight.

When we reach Jackson Square, there's a small crowd collected around a pair of dueling violinists. Both Jeffrey and I naturally gravitate in that direction. The music is hypnotic, but it's when we get close enough to see the couple that I'm truly mesmerized. The guy is tall and lanky, just how I like 'em. He's got light caramel skin, and a fluff of springy curls atop his head. And his eyes...I'm getting vagina flutters just witnessing the way he's fucking the willowy brunette with those mossy green orbs.

There's so much passion in the way the two of them play that I can't help but imagine what'll be going down in their room tonight. If they make it that far. I kinda hope he goes all caveman and fucks her right here where we can watch. A girl can dream, right?

"Aren't they beautiful?" I ask Jeffrey, who hasn't said a word. It's the longest he's gone without talking since we left the strip club.

"You think they're a couple?" he asks, moving his hand to the small of my back. Goosebumps breakout across my skin as he glides his thumb back and forth.

I nod. "Have to be. Strangers don't look at each other like that, CEO."

We watch in silence for the rest of their set, and I wonder if Jeff's body is having the same physical reaction as mine. I feel hot and needy—bordering on desperate—and I *just* had two orgasms. "I bet if they performed outside of the sex toy shop, they'd sell the place out."

"You ready to go again, Tink?"

"God, yes."

The music stops, and the beautiful couple instantly fall into one another's arms, making out like it's their life source. I wonder what it's like to feel a love so intense.

Jeff releases my hand, stumbling over to the tip bucket and dropping a wad of cash inside. "Thanks for warming my girl up for me," he says at a volume much louder than his usual speaking voice. Then he returns to my side, grabbing my hand and heading in the direction of the café.

My girl. He called me his girl. I know it was nothing more than an alcohol-induced slip of the tongue, but I'm confused as fuck at why this isn't sending me running for the hills. Why'd I like hearing those two words so much? Most of all, why is there suddenly the tiniest part of me that wishes he meant it?

"Where're you going, Jeff?" He's suddenly pulling me in the direction of some creepy little alley. "The café is that way."

He points ahead to a dimly lit table in the back of the alleyway. It's then that I notice the sign, "Lady Adelaide's psychic readings."

"Oh, no." Turning back the way we came, I tug on his arm. "I'm not doing this shit, Jeffrey. I told you that already."

"I'll do it. It'll be fun. Come on, Tink." I have a *really* bad feeling about this, but he's so damn eager and cute and I can't tell him no.

"Fine. But I'm just watching."

"Deal."

Lady Adelaide has a fancy setup compared to the others we've passed by, most of which were just a simple black folding table with a handmade posterboard sign taped to the front. This chick has a legit banner and thick purple drapes on rods which she closes around us for privacy. There's an odd scent... some sort of incense is burning, and the smoke only adds to the creepy atmosphere. I can't believe Jeffrey's into this shit.

"Hi. Welcome." A beautiful Creole woman with the most amazing creamy mocha skin and hypnotic green eyes greets us with a smile. "I'm Lady Adelaide...Are we here for a couple's reading tonight?"

"Oh, no." I shake my head, motioning to Jeffrey. "We're not a couple."

Her forehead crinkles. "No?" She looks from me to the CEO and back again with a knowing glance. I think she may have just winked at me. *How weird.*

"No," Jeff agrees, sitting in the chair opposite hers. "We're definitely just friends."

Lady Adelaide nods, although she's clearly not convinced. "All right, so here's what we're going to do Mr....?"

"Jeff."

"Jeff." She nods. "I want you to hold this deck of cards in your hands and think about your life. Where you've been. Where you are now. Where you're going. Any concerns you may have for your future. I want you to put your energy into that deck for me, Mr. Jeff."

He takes the big clunky deck of worn cards from her hands. His eyes close, and he's silent for a moment before handing them back.

"Very good. Now I want you to choose five cards," she says, fanning them out across the table. "One at a time."

Jeffrey begins picking out cards and handing them to Adelaide, who arranges them in the shape of a cross in the center of the table. He looks over to me and winks.

"Very good." She nods, studying the spread.

As she starts to read his cards, my stomach grows weak. Lady Adelaide mentions a great love from his past, and how he's still struggling with that loss. Jeffrey nods, his face going white and eyes glistening in the candlelight, and suddenly this fun and frivolous adventure becomes so much more than we bargained for.

"This card tells me that you've reached a very important crossroads, Mr. Jeffrey. Whatever happened in your past is preventing you from living your life. It's preventing you from moving forward."

Jeff coughs, clearing his throat. "My wife," he finally says, breaking down. "I lost my wife."

Lady Adelaide rests a hand over his, gently. "I'm very sorry for your loss."

My heart twists into knots. I can't handle seeing him in so much pain. I want to grab him by the arm and drag him out of here, putting an end to this torture. Why would anyone willingly submit themselves to this?

"Ahh. But this card here tells me that a beautiful future awaits you. A soulmate, Mr. Jeffrey. And I'm getting the feeling you've already met this person." Her brows raise in question.

I swear the man turns white as a sheet. It's not even my reading, and I'm freaking shaking. He doesn't utter a word. Just sits there growing paler by the minute.

"You have a lot to think about. Find a way to deal with your pain, or this new life may never come to fruition. Many people spend their whole lives searching for their soulmates. You're one of the lucky few to have been blessed with two. This is a good fortune, Mr. Jeffrey. Don't let it slip away."

"Can I ask what happened?" I work up the nerve to ask after a mostly silent walk to his hotel from the card reading. We're about to step inside, and I know that once we do there will be little chance for talking. "How'd she—"

"Yeah. No...it's fine. She died after giving birth to Willow." His hand scrubs over his face, and he stumbles a little on the uneven sidewalk.

"Oh my God, Jeffrey. I'm so sorry. Did she ever get the chance to see her?" I ask, while reaching for his arm to steady him.

"You don't have to apologize, Tink. It's not your fault." He gives my hand a gentle squeeze, as if he's trying to console me. "Yeah, she saw her. I have a few pictures of them in the hospital, actually. They're the last pictures we have of her. She passed away a few hours after Willow was born. Jess was asleep, and I'd gone down to the nursery to check on the baby. When I got back to the room—" His face takes on a faraway look, and I can tell he's reliving the awful event.

"It's okay," I say rubbing his back when I see how upset he's become. "I shouldn't have asked."

"I found her—" he stops walking, biting down on his knuckle, and lets out a guttural cry. "Lying in a pool of blood on the—on the floor."

My hand lifts to cover my mouth and warm tears line my cheeks as my heart breaks into a million tiny pieces for this man, who lost the love of his life. For Willow, who will never know her mother. For Jessica, who will never get the chance to see what a true joy her baby girl is. And for Evangeline, who had to go through such a traumatic loss at way too young of an age.

"They tried to revive her," he continues. "But it was too late. She—She'd lost too much blood."

"Jeffrey," I say, reaching my hands up to touch his face, smoothing his tears away with my thumbs. His pain is palpable, reaching deep within my bones.

He doesn't say another word. Just stares into my eyes. I'm experiencing a connection the likes of which I've ever felt before. It's as if I can finally really *see* this man. Truly see him, right down to his soul, and it terrifies me just how much I like what I see.

I'm a little unsure if it's the right move to make when I pull his face down, bringing his lips to mine. I kiss him softly. Tenderly. It takes Jeff a moment to respond, and I'm afraid he's about to push me away, but his lips part and his tongue brushes against mine. It's velvety soft and tastes of whiskey. Jeffrey takes his time savoring every stroke, every breath, every touch.

Knotting his fingers into my hair, he holds me close, as if he's afraid I'll disappear. "I need to get you upstairs," he rasps against my lips, and my heart damn near convulses in my chest.

It takes me a moment to come down from the cloud I'm floating on. "Lead the way."

The ride in the elevator up to the twenty-sixth floor is excruciating. I don't know which is fluttering faster, my heart or my nether region. I want another taste of what we started downstairs, but the elevator is packed, so I have to settle for discreet touches. A brush of his hand on my backside. The feathering of his lips at my temple. His warm breath on my neck.

When we finally reach our floor and make it into Jeffrey's

hotel room, I'm all wound up and overly emotional.

"Gina," he growls, backing me up against the hotel room door. His hands are on my face, his thumbs tracing my jawline, my neck, my collarbone. "Thank you for today," he rasps, hitting me with another one of his soul-deep stares. "I needed this." His head shakes, and he lets out a resigned breath. "I needed *you* more than I realized."

"Jeffrey," I mewl, unsure of how to respond to such declarations. My heart is racing, my pussy throbbing, and there's something else—something foreign—and it's making me all warm and tingly. "I *still* need you."

He chuckles as I rub myself up against him, and I'm glad I can lighten his mood a little. I hate seeing him hurt. "You really have a thing for my dick, don't you?"

"God, yes." I reach for his button, unfastening his pants, and they fall to the floor with a thud.

"Slow down, babe. My wallet is in my pocket. I need a condom."

I don't know what comes over me in that moment, but I want to do something with him I've never done with another man. He's shared so much of himself today, and I want to give him something in return. "I want you to fuck me bare," I say, lifting my dress over my head and tossing it to the floor.

His jaw drops, "Gina, I don't...I mean, I obviously have, but not since..."

Panic wells in my chest, and I press my finger to his lips. "Please, don't go there. Not now, Jeffrey." If he says her name in this moment, I will run home crying like a horny-ass baby. "If you don't want to, it's fine. I just thought...Well, I've never done it before without a condom, and it was just an idea."

He worries his lip between his teeth, his eyes roaming up

and down the length of my body. "Are you sure?"

Nodding, I rub my hands over his chest. "I had a hysterectomy, Jeff. It's impossible for me to get pregnant, and I swear I'm clean."

"You trust me?" he asks, incredulous.

"You're the most responsible man I've ever met, and the only one I've ever trusted enough."

My words seem to flip a switch in him. Jeff scoops me into his arms, carrying me over to the bed where he gently lays me across the middle. Before joining me, he removes the rest of his clothing. The bedside lamp is the only light in the room, and it's on just long enough for me to get a glimpse of the light spattering of hair on his chest that runs down to a mouthwatering happy trail, pointing straight to the promised land, before Jeff switches it off on his way into bed.

"You're so beautiful, Tink, lying in my bed with your hair spread over my pillow like that," he says, crawling in to rest beside me. He trails one finger along the bend of my neck, over the tops of my breasts, down the center of my tummy, finally skimming the waist of my suit bottom.

My entire body comes alive beneath the tenderness in his touch. "No one's ever touched me like that," I admit, squirming a little.

"With a finger?"

"With their heart."

Chapter Nineteen

JEFFREY

I wake from a dead sleep with vomit rising in my throat. The smell of alcohol seeping from my pores only increases the urge to hurl. Swallowing hard, I pull in deep breaths—a weak attempt to ward off the inevitable and inhale a mouthful of hair.

Hair? What the fuck?

"Mmm," an unmistakably female voice moans, shifting her naked body further on top of mine. I wrap my arm around her, pulling her close, but it feels all wrong. My Jess was tall and curvy, with hair that stopped at her shoulders. The locks I just pulled from my mouth extend well past the too-small tits resting against my chest. She stirs again, and I get a whiff of strawberries and tequila. *Tink.* The day before flashes like a movie reel in my mind. The party at Dillon's house, brunch, the strip club, the sex. More sex. Incredible fucking sex. The psychic—what a fucking disaster.

I reach for my phone, bringing it to my face to check the time. Just after 6:30 in the morning.

She stayed the night.

Son of a bitch. Whatever progress I'd made at pushing down the bile in my throat is gone. I throw her off me, tripping over our discarded shoes and clothing as I feel my way through the dark, unfamiliar hotel room to the bathroom and fall to my knees, emptying the contents of my stomach into the toilet.

"What the fuck, Jeffrey?" I hear Gina shout from the bed. "You almost tossed me right onto the—oh. Oh, are you all right?" Day-old booze sprays from my mouth and nose with violent force. I can't stop myself to answer.

Tap. Tap. Tap. I feel her presence lurking in the doorway. "Do you need anything?" There she goes, trying to take care of me again. I told her I didn't want a girlfriend. What happened between us last night meant nothing.

"Out. Get. Out!" I manage to roar between retching.

"Whatever," the very embodiment of regret grumbles from behind me, still naked. "I'm going back to bed."

"Out!" I shout, as my heart twists up into knots.

Gina gasps, loudly, but I can't bring myself to turn around and face her. "Are you kicking me out? Like out, out?"

My eyes burn with unshed tears as a wave of guilt threatens to suffocate me. I haven't spent the night with another woman since my wife. And what we did—what I remember of last night— was so much more than fucking. "Please, go."

"You know what? Fuck you, Jeffrey. Fuck you for treating me like a fucking whore." She spits a string of curses that I more than deserve as she rushes around the room, throwing on her clothes and collecting her belongings.

"Jessica," I moan into the bowl. I can't remember ever feeling this awful.

"Newsflash, CEO," Gina shouts as she walks past. "She's

dead!" The door slams shut.

AFTER A FEW HOURS, A steaming hot shower, and a cruise around town to clear my head, I'm parking my gray Tundra in Gramma Betty's pea-pebble drive.

"Well, ain't you a sight for sore eyes," Jessica's elderly mother observes, not even trying to hide her amusement. "I take it you had a good time last night?"

With a shrug of my shoulders, I place a kiss to her cheek and step inside. "It was okay. How were the girls?"

"They was just fine. Like always."

"Daddy!" Willow shouts as she comes barreling through the house, her bare feet slapping on the wood floor. She wraps her arms and legs around my calf, sitting on the top of my foot, and I give her a ride, dragging her along with me to the kitchen. Her peals of laughter brighten my mood considerably.

"Did you have fun with Gramma, baby girl?"

"We haded a tea pawty and Nina and Becky came sweepover too." Nina and Becky are their cousins on Jess's side. Her brother Jacob's kids. They don't see each other near as often as they used to, and I feel bad about that, but I just couldn't bring myself to continue living in a town where I see my wife at every turn.

"That sounds amazing." After untangling her from my leg, I lift my mini-me into my lap and brush back her mass of blonde curls with my hand, raining kisses along her forehead and cheeks. "I missed you, princess."

"You didn't tell me Evangeline was seeing someone." Betty's tone is accusing.

"They met on the cruise last month and talk on the phone.

That hardly constitutes dating."

She shrugs. "Vangie seems to think he's her boyfriend," Betty singsongs with a small smirk. The woman loved to rile me up.

"Impossible." I wipe my sweaty palms on my jeans and send Willow for her brush.

The old woman crosses her arms on her chest, tapping her slippered foot on the floor with amusement in her eyes. "Why's that impossible?"

"Cuz I never said she could have a boyfriend."

When my little girl returns with her bag, I fish out the brush and ponytail holders, working my lingering frustration out on the knots. Ignoring Betty's chuckle, I begin parting Willow's hair into two pieces and then put each side up into a high ponytail, just the way Vangie taught me. "There," I say, swatting her on the bottom to send her off to play. "Much better."

"What happened last night?" my mother-in-law asks, once Willow is out of the room. "Something's bothering you, I can tell."

"It's nothing," I lie, not wanting to get into how confused I am over my feelings for a woman who is not my wife—who is not her daughter.

"All she ever wanted was for you to be happy, you know?" Damn this woman for being able to read me so well. Guess that's what happens when you've known someone for as long as we've known each other.

A wad of emotion rises in my throat. "I know." And I do. We had the conversation multiple times during our many years together, about how we'd want each other to move on if anything ever happened to one of us. But when we said those things, I never imagined it would ever become my reality. It's not like she and I parted on bad terms. I'm in love with that woman today as much as I ever was. That's why whatever is happening with Tink has me all fucked up.

"She's not coming back, Jeffrey." Betty walks over, rubbing her hand along my upper back. "Whatever happened...it's okay."

"What's wrong?" Vangie's face is filled with concern as she walks in on her grandmother and me in a tearful embrace.

"Everything's fine, baby. Come give Daddy a hug. I missed you."

My big girl walks over hesitantly, still trying to figure out what she's missing. When she wraps her arms around my neck and hugs me tight, she whispers, "He is so my boyfriend."

"Is not."

"Yep," she argues, popping the p as she walks over to the counter and grabs an apple from the fruit basket. "He's a great kisser, too."

The urge to vomit has suddenly returned. "You're grounded."

Vangie glares at me then takes a bite and smirks. "Am not."

ON OUR WAY HOME, WE make our routine stop at Guidry's, the local flower shop. Willow picks out her usual bouquet of pink roses, and this time Evangeline chooses a spring mix. I grab the biggest bouquet of red roses I can find and drive over to the cemetery for a picnic with Jessica.

I know that probably sounds morbid. I promise that I haven't fallen off the deep end. Before Jessica died, we used to take Evangeline to the park for a picnic every Sunday after church. On the day of her funeral, my little girl asked if we could come back here to have a picnic with Mommy since she wouldn't be able to come to the park. It didn't matter how creepy or weird it made me, my baby had just lost her mother, and there was no way in hell I was going to tell her no. Since then, without fail, one Sunday a month, we come out to visit Jessica. I think it's been a positive thing for the girls—a way for us all to feel close to her. For Willow to have some form of relationship with her.

"Tum fine me Daddy," Willow yells from somewhere in the graveyard.

"Willow, we don't play around the graves. Come out and finish your sandwich."

"Fine, den. I jus gonna stay hiding til Mom fines me," she threatens.

Evangeline rolls her eyes. "She's dead, sissy. Mom's not coming to find you." *Ouch*. There's that word again. I feel like I've been beat over the head during the past twenty-four hours with reminders of the fact that my wife is gone for good. Someone definitely wants me to get that memo.

"It's not fair," Willow whines, coming out from behind a large tomb and making her way back to join us on the blanket. "I never get to pway wif Mommy. Vangie gotted to."

"I'm sorry, princess. I'll play with you when we get home, okay? It's just disrespectful to play in the cemetery." It takes all the strength I can muster not to fall to fucking pieces in front of my girls.

Godamn it. Does this ever get easier?

"I don't wanna pway wif you again. I want my mommy."

Me too, pumpkin. Me too.

Chapter Twenty

GINA

"Well, hello there, sunshine." Cooper welcomes me with a huge grin that's just oozing sarcasm when I burst through the front door of their house.

"Don't start with me," I warn, pointing my finger at him. "Spencerrrrrr!" I shout. "I need you. It's an emergency!"

"She's upstairs investigating a drive-by shaving." Coop's eyes roll when her voice echoes down the stairwell.

"Oh, shit," I groan. "I'm going in."

A soft chuckle follows. "Good luck. I'm gonna hang down here and *watch* the babies." He gestures to the sleeping infants in the bassinet, making air quotes. "And maintain safe distance away from *that*." His eyes point upward.

Taking the stairs two at a time, I rush over to see what my sister-wife is screaming about. *How dare she have a crisis coinciding with mine? Doesn't she know I need her?*

"Which one of you did it?" she asks, pointing to the rug of pubes lining her tub... er sanctuary. "And don't try to blame

Coop. It wasn't him...I checked."

Lake and Landon each point a finger at the other. "Wasn't me."

Oh, this is gonna be good, I think, bracing myself against the doorframe, ready to watch this thing play out.

"Don't think I won't make him come up here and check," my deranged friend threatens.

"You can't make me do it!" Coop shouts from the bottom of the stairs.

"You both know very well that I can make him do anything," Spence grits between clenched teeth. "Fess up."

Lake tugs the top of his basketball shorts down a fraction of an inch. "See, Mom? I didn't do it. The trail of tears is still fully intact."

"Uh, excuse me," I interject, stepping into the room, finally making my presence known. "It's called a *happy trail.*"

"Oh, no, Aunt Gina. One day when some lucky lady, whoever she may be, gets her eyes on what I'm packin'...There will be tears of joy, or pain." He shrugs then smirks.

"Oh, God." Spencer rolls her eyes with exasperation. "I don't even know how to deal with this shit." She waves her hand, gesturing to the teen boys who are doing their best to give my best friend a heart attack before they reach adulthood.

"Fine," Landon pipes up, hanging his head in shame. "It was me."

"Why the hell are you—you know what? It's probably best if you don't answer that. Just know this," she says, getting up on her toes to get as close to eye level as she can manage. She'd be better off standing on the toilet seat at this point. "I have access to all of your text messages, and if your porno nuts pop up in the texts between you and Evangeline...I cannot be held responsible for my actions."

"I'm no—"

"I don't want to hear another word. Now find a way to get that shit out of my bathtub, and you'd better not miss a single one." Spencer gags. "And don't rinse it down the drain, or you'll be the one explaining to the plumber why he's pulling your pubes out of the pipes."

"Never a dull moment around here, is there?" I ask, trying not to be an asshole and laugh. She's really pissed. I'll make fun of her later.

"Hey, Gina." She walks over to give me a squeeze, and I can feel her heart racing from exertion.

"You need to calm down, Spence. You just gave birth five weeks ago. This can't be good for you, Momma."

"I know...they just make me so damn crazy sometimes, Gina. I mean, they know they aren't allowed in my bathroom, for one." She eyes the two delinquent boys.

Lake throws his hands up. "Hey, don't look at me."

"And you never asked if you could shave your balls," she adds pointedly at Landon.

"Hey. You never said I couldn't."

Shrug. "The boy kinda has a point."

"Traitor," she whisper-hisses. "He at least could have cleaned up the fucking evidence. It's like when they were little—" A huge grin lights her face. *Squirrel!* "Remember? When they first learned to write, and they'd graffiti the walls and furniture?"

Oh, how I miss those days. "And they always swore it wasn't them," I finish her thought. "But the little fuckers always wrote their own names."

The twins' cheeks turn an identical shade of red.

"They weren't even smart enough to write each others' names," Spence adds, laughing.

I really worried about the two of them. "How you've managed to make honor roll all these years still blows my mind."

"Ha-ha," Landon mocks. "Someday we'll be the ones taking care of you two hags on our doctors' salaries."

"When did you start allowing them to speak to us like this, Spence?"

"I didn't."

"Serious talk," I say, looking to each of the boys. "You two need to cut this shit out. Stop stressing your momma out like this. You should be helping her right now. Don't make Aunt Gigi come over here and whoop your little...er, big asses. 'Cuz I will totally go Gina circa 2010." I snap my fingers in an exaggerated fashion. "Like that."

"Yes, ma'am," Lake mutters, trying not to laugh.

Landon takes a step toward his mother giving her a big hug. "Sorry, Mom."

"Sorry for what?" I ask, the way I have since they were little. *I'm sorry* are only words unless you know what you're apologizing for.

His cheeks flush. "For defiling your tub," he mutters.

"And?" I stare him down.

"Uhh. Shaving without asking?" he answers, his brows dipped in uncertainty.

"All right now," I say, opening my arms and waggling my fingers. "Come give Auntie her hugs. I've missed you little shits."

⚜

"So, TELL ME HOW IT went seeing Dillon yesterday. Judging by your face, not well?" my best friend asks, plopping down beside me on the white wicker swing on her front porch.

Seeing Dillon? Was that just yesterday? In the midst of the tidal wave that was running into Jeffrey again, I'd completely pushed that disaster to the back of my mind. "Oh, uh. That was awful."

"Is that not what you came here to talk about?"

"Honestly, I'd forgotten all about his dumb ass, with how the rest of my day went."

Spence pulls one leg up, folding it under her bottom, and turns to face me. "Tell me everything."

So, I start by telling her about Dillon and Clarissa, and how she jumped on my ass at Aunt Martha's in front of everyone.

"She didn't?" Spencer's mouth falls open in shock. "What a cunt...Please tell me you kicked her ass, bestie?"

My blood is heating just thinking about it. "Well, here's the thing, I was about to when Jeffrey was suddenly just standing there, staring, and then the bitch sucker-punched me while I was hypnotized by his stupid handsome face."

Her thumb rubs under my right eye. "Right here, I'm guessing? You're starting to bruise."

With a wince, I push her hand off. "That hurts."

"Sorry."

"Jeffrey..." I widen my eyes for emphasis. "He's the guy from the cruise."

Spencer's eyes get round. "Oh my God. Evangeline's dad? I hadn't...shit. What did you do?"

"What do you think I did? What I always do. I fucked him in the laundry room."

Spence snickers. "You are such a slut...So, the day wasn't a total loss then, right?" She waggles her brows with exaggeration. "Bow chicka bow wow."

"Girl, I am just getting started."

I proceed to fill her in on the rest of our day, all the way up to the most amazing sexual experience of my life.

She pulls her bottom lip between her teeth, chewing nervously. "So, you like him then...like *really* like him."

"Fuck, no." I shake my head. "I hate him."

"But you just said...I thought..."

"Momentary lapse in sanity. I'm not myself when I'm horny."

Spence spits out a laugh. "Uh, yeah you are. You are your truest self when you're horny, hooker."

"Maybe..."

"There's more, isn't there? What's got you all upset?"

My eyes start to burn with unwelcome tears. "He—umm." One salty drop manages to sneak out and drips down my cheek. *Fuck him.* "He kicked me out. Like, we spent the most amazing night together...I mean, he told me about his dead wife, Spencer. Then, he woke up hungover, and—mid-puke—started yelling at me to get out. It's like he was disgusted by my presence. Most humiliating moment of my life. I have never been thrown out on my ass by a man before."

"Oh, Gina." My bestie's eyes well up with sympathy.

"Nuh-uh. It was just a stupid mistake on my part. I knew we were never going to be anything more than sex. That was the deal all along. I fucked up and caught some feelings, but I'm throwing that shit back. Done."

"There's a great man out there somewhere who's going to sweep you off your feet someday, Gina, and I can't wait."

"I don't want to be swept off my feet, Spence. I like my feet safely rooted to the ground."

Chapter Twenty-One

JEFFREY

"Mr. Ryan?" Angie, my secretary calls through the intercom speaker in my office.

"Yeah?"

"There's a Kinsey calling for you on line one. I told her you were very busy today and didn't have time for social calls, just like you've instructed, but she insisted you'd want to talk to her."

Goddamn it. Kinsey is the girl I'd been casually hooking up with before Gina blew into my world like a fucking tornado, turning my life upside down. I've been dodging Kinsey's calls to my cell for weeks. Now she's tracking me down at my office? She's persistent, I'll give her that. "Go ahead and put her through, Angie. Thank you."

"No problem, Mr. Ryan."

"This is Jeff."

"Finally," she sighs. "You're a hard man to get ahold of, Jeffrey."

"Yes, well, I'm a busy man, Kinsey. I told you that."

"I know…It's just—well, it's been a while, and I was hoping maybe we could meet up tonight for a quickie?" She doesn't beat around the bush, does she? It was what I'd originally liked about her. Wham, bam, thank you ma'am. It was exactly what I thought I needed, before *her*.

"Tonight won't work for me."

"Okay, well, what day is good for you? I'm pretty open." *No shit?*

"Kinsey, I'm actually going through some things right now, and sex is the furthest thing from my mind."

That's such bullshit. Sex is pretty much the only thing on my mind. Sex in a moon chair…sex at the strip club…sex with a sassy little blonde I can't manage to get out of my fucking head.

"Oh…Well, you don't think that maybe it would help get your mind off of whatever's bothering you?"

"No. I don't."

"Is there someone else?" Oh, fuck. Here we go.

"Kinsey?"

"Yeah?"

"You do understand that there was never a you and me, right?"

"Oh, sure…Yes, of course." She doesn't sound all that convinced.

"Great. So, there's no one *else*, because there is and never was an *us*. There is someone though, and she's the reason this isn't going to happen anymore."

"But, I thought you said you didn't do relationships. If that's what you wanted…"

"I don't. It's not. Listen, I've got another call coming in that I'm going to have to answer. You take care, okay?"

I miss Gina, I finally admit to myself when I hang up with

Kinsey. Dammit, do I ever fucking miss her, but that doesn't change the fact that I can't have her. As much as it hurts to acknowledge it, she got under my skin, but I'm not looking for a relationship. I will *never* remarry. My girls had a mother, and I'm not looking to fill that void.

My stomach twists into knots when I remember the pained look on her face when our eyes met for the last time. Gina talks a good game, but I know that I hurt her, even if she'd never admit it.

My fist comes down hard on the top of my desk, rattling its contents. I can't believe I lost it on her like that.

I'm going to have to find a way to get over this...whatever *this* is.

"Damn, you home early," Willow says when I walk through the door just after noon. I cringe.

"What did I tell you about that word?" I ask, bending to lift her into my arms.

"Not to say dat."

"Ladies don't talk like that, Willow. You want to be a lady, right?"

"Dat's not true, Daddy. Gigi says sentence hancers, and she's a bootiful wady."

I can't escape her, even in my own home. "She is very beautiful. Whether or not she's a lady...Well, that's questionable," I mutter, setting her back to her feet.

"Hey, Dad."

"Hey, sweet pea. How was Willow today?"

"She was fine."

"Oh, Daddy," Willow says, tugging on the bottom of my shirt for my attention. "I gotted to talk to Tyle today on FaceTime!" she squeals.

"Did you?"

"Mmhmm," she nods. "Sissy talls dem boys every day when you go to work."

"Well, that explains your language lately," I tease, eyeing Evangeline.

"They're good kids, Daddy." She sighs, dramatically.

"I know, or I wouldn't allow you to talk to them. I do wish you two wouldn't pick up their bad habits, however."

Her green eyes roll back in her head. "Damn is hardly even a curse word anymore, Daddy."

"According to who?"

She shrugs. "Everyone. Everyone elses' parents let them say it."

"Well then, it's a *damn* good thing you aren't being raised by everyone elses' parents."

"Hardy-har. What're you doing home so early, anyway?"

Shrug. "I didn't have much going on at the office today and figured I'd come pick you two up to go shopping...but if you'd rather hang out here, I'm sure I can go find something at the office to keep me busy."

"Wait here...I'll go get my purse."

AFTER *DAMN* NEAR FIVE HOURS at the mall with Vangie and Willow, in a failed attempt to distract myself from thoughts of Gina, all I managed to do was come home about a thousand dollars poorer. *Sigh.* Well, at least my girls are excited about their new wardrobes.

It's creeping on midnight now, and I'm still tossing and turning. Guilt is a son of a bitch. Maybe if I found a way to contact her and apologize for my barbaric behavior the other day, I'd be able to move on.

Chapter Twenty-Two

GINA

It's almost eight o'clock when I finish up with my final client for the day. I can't wait til Spence returns to work in a couple more weeks, because these late nights are cramping my style. I haven't been out—haven't had sex—since the Fourth of July.

Well, tonight I'm going to put an end to this drought. It's been two weeks, and I think a good hookup is just what I need to cure my sour mood.

"GINAAA, LONG TIME NO SEE, babe. Where ya been?" My little bartender bestie, Will, asks as I stroll in to Partners, my old stomping grounds. This is where I come when I'm craving some cock. Located a few towns over in Whiskey Falls, it keeps the gossipmongers somewhat off my ass, or at the very least ...their sons out of my bed.

"Ugh." With a groan, I saddle up to the bar. "Work, work,

work. I'm running the office alone until Spence is back from maternity leave, and it's kicking my ass."

"My poor little pixie," he croons, setting a shot of Fireball in front of me. "My treat."

"Thanks, babe." As the warm liquid glides down my throat, all I can see is that CEO's stupid smiling face and those damn crow's feet that do inexplicable things to my girlie parts. *Fuck*. One more reason to hate him. Jeffrey Ryan has ruined my favorite shot. It will forever be tainted by memories of our time spent together in NOLA.

"Feel better?" sweet William asks, his blond brows dipped inward with concern.

"Can you get me a shot of tequila to wash it down?" I ask my flamboyant friend, who eyes me skeptically.

"Honey, are you sure? You always have Fireball. You hate tequila."

"Sometimes peoples' tastes change."

"Touché."

After three more shots, Will leans across the bar, "So, did you select your victim of the night?"

My eyes make another pass around the room but no one is particularly sticking out to me. "Meh," I shrug. "You choose."

Will's hand lifts to his chest. "Me? Why you've never let me choose your *cock*tail before. Are you sure you're feeling okay?"

"Yeah. Just pick one." The hunt is something I always enjoyed in the past, but tonight I just wanna scratch this itch and go home.

He rubs his hands together and squeals. "This is so exciting. I've never gotten to choose from the straight pool before."

This boy is a mess. "Just pick one already. I need some ass so I can go to bed."

"That one," Will says, pointing to a guy over at the pool tables.

"I guess he'll do."

"He'll do? Honey, did you see that tight ass? Watch him. Watch the next time he bends over. Boy can work a stick, too. I bet he's real good with his dick."

"God, I hope so," I say winking at my friend as I get up from my chair and make my way over to the tables. He's got big shoes to fill.

"Hey there," I say, walking up to the tall, dark, muscled hunk that Will picked out for me. My friend knows my tastes well. "I've been watching you play for a while from the bar and was wondering if maybe you could give me some tips?"

Whiskey eyes rove over my body, assessing the goods. "Sure thing, cutie." His hand darts out for mine. "I'm Russ. What's your name?"

"Gina."

"Well, Gina, the most important thing I do is use a lot of cue silk."

"Uh-huh," I say, feigning interest. "And what's that do?"

"It lubricates the shaft." Russ slides his hand up and down the pool stick suggestively. "My game is always better when my shaft is super slippery."

Oh, gawd. I think I just threw up in my mouth. "How long have you been waiting to use that line, Russ?"

His cheeks flush. "It was good, right?"

"I'm going to be frank with you. It didn't do it for me."

"Uh, okay," the meathead says, looking around in confusion. I mean, how did a line that good fail him, right?

"Listen, I'm just going to give it to you straight because I'm getting too old for this shit and have to be at work early in the morning."

"Okay."

"So, I'm just interested in hooking up. One time. No strings. I don't even want your number, and no, before you ask, you can't have mine."

His eyes light up like a kid in a candy store. "Are you even real?"

WE'RE OUTSIDE, BEHIND THE BAR, my back pressed up against the bricks, and Russ's hand starts to creep up my shirt. When he cups my breast, my entire body tenses. It feels foreign. It feels wrong. Then his mouth lowers to meet mine, and instinctively my head turns.

"What's wrong?" Russ asks, pressing his erection into my stomach as he continues to paw at my breasts.

"Nothing," I lie, trying to force myself to get into it. I run my hands over his muscled chest, his broad shoulders. Russ's body is truly amazing, and for some reason it's doing less than nothing for me. Scratch that—I know the reason, and it's fucking pissing me off. I can do this. I can get over Jeff Ryan.

When his hand wanders lower and cups my pussy, I panic, pushing him off of me.

"Whoa." He backs away, throwing his hands up in the air. "What the—?"

"I'm sorry," I whisper, breaking out in a cold sweat. My pulse is racing, and I can hardly stand upright with how badly my body is shaking.

"Look, I don't know what's going on here, but you practically threw yourself at me." He looks worried, like I might accuse him of doing something wrong.

"I—I know. I'm sorry. I wanted to. I don't know what happened."

His hand combs through his brown locks, his frustration morphing into concern. "Should I call someone?"

"No. I'm fine," I stammer. "I just need a minute. I'll be fine."

"You sure?" His face is uncertain as he starts to walk back toward the door.

"Yeah. I'm just gonna go home. I'm really sorry for all of this."

He nods. "I'll be all right, Gina. Get home safe, okay?" Then, he dips his head, pulling the heavy door open.

Once he disappears back into the bar, I make a beeline for my car.

AFTER A NICE, WARM BUBBLE bath, I curl up in bed, ready to dive into the book Spencer hasn't shut up about. Who even am I right now? Passing on sex for a romance novel? *Oh, how far the sexy have fallen.*

Reaching over to the bedside table, I switch on the lamp and pull the paperback from the drawer. *Coming Up Roses* by LK Farlow.

Before I know it, hours have gone by. I keep telling myself just one more chapter, but it's like starting a new series on Netflix. I'm binging...a book!

I'm about three-fourths of the way through and arguing with myself about whether or not I actually need to get any sleep before work tomorrow, when my text message alert pings.

Unknown: Hey Tink. It's me...Jeffrey. I hope it's okay that I tricked Dillon into giving me your number. I may have told him I misplaced it, but I feel really horrible about how we left things the other day.

How *we* left things? Before I can hand him his ass via text, another message comes through, causing my heart to skip a beat.

Unknown: When I woke up and you were still there, I just...Well, I panicked. You didn't deserve to be treated that way and I need to apologize. I'm really sorry, Gina. I never meant to hurt you. I'm so fucked up.

At least he has a valid reason to be fucked up. I just ran out on poor Russ after whoring myself all over him.

Me: Jeffrey...I wish I could hate you for so much more than your little meltdown the other morning, but I can't. You broke me. You and your wondercock. I can't even fuck anymore. I'm READING!

Jeffrey: Wondercock, eh? I kinda like that. What are you reading?

Me: A romance novel Spence has been after me to read for a while now. I tried to hook up with this guy and I totally freaked out, ran home, and curled up in bed, but couldn't sleep. I decided I'd give it a try and now I can't put it down.

Jeffrey: He misses you too.

Me: Who?

Jeffrey: Wondercock.

Me: Are we going to do anything about it?

Jeffrey: Can I call you?

Me: Sure

Chapter Twenty-Three

JEFFREY

"Hello?" Gina's sleepy voice is even grittier than usual and gets my blood pumping.

"Tink, it's good to hear your voice." My entire body seems to sigh with relief. The tension that's been lingering for the past few days just evaporates.

"Is it?"

"More than you know."

"What are you doing, CEO?" Her loud sigh echoes through the phone.

"I had a good time with you the other day." It's more difficult than it should be to admit that to myself least of all to her. A ball of nerves gets lodged in my throat as I await her reply.

"I could tell." Her words ooze sarcasm. It'll be a long time before I live this down, but that's okay. I deserve her ire after being such a dick to her.

"This isn't easy for me, Tink..."

Her throat clears. "I know. I'm sorry. Go on, I'm listening."

"It just hit me hard. I never expected to actually *wan*

to be with another woman...I have all this guilt. Logically, I know that she'd want me to be happy, but I can't shake this sick feeling that I'm doing something wrong." Dammit. I'm rambling already. I scrub a hand over my face and sigh. "I want to see you again, and not just to have sex with you...although I really, really want that too." I have a semi just thinking of being with her again.

"I don't know, Jeffrey. What's going to happen the next time you have a gut check? I realize you're going through a lot. I can't even imagine what you're feeling, but I won't be your punching bag."

"I'm a selfish bastard for asking this of you, and I'll completely understand if it's too much. But, I want you in the only way I'm capable. I want your body. I want your friendship. I won't ask for your heart, because I can't give you mine, Tink."

"That's cool. I only want you for your cock anyway."

I shake my head, laughing into the phone. "So, does that mean we're doing this?"

"If *this* is each other then I say hell to the yeah!"

"Would it be too much to ask that we're exclusive?" I press. "I've never done well with sharing my toys."

"Well, my shit won't work for anyone else anyway, so that shouldn't be a problem."

"Can we be serious here for a second, Tink?"

"Okay," she breathes out softly, almost inaudibly.

"If it gets to be too much, I want you to tell me, and if someone else comes along, I want you to let me go. Promise you won't let me keep you from what you deserve, because you deserve so much more than this."

"I'm damaged goo—"

"Stop," I growl. "I don't want to hear that shit. I want you to tell me that you understand. That you're not going into this with any false pretenses, and that you'll keep an open mind. The right guy just may sneak up on you when you least expect it and I don't want you missing out on him for me."

"Yeah, okay..."

"Promise."

"I promise."

We're both silent for a long pause, before I speak up. "So, when can I see you, Tink?"

"I don't know, CEO...I'm not sure how this works. What's allowed? What are we telling *people*?"

By *people* I know she means my kids. I hadn't really thought that far out. I don't want them thinking I'm trying to replace their mother. This is hard enough for me to accept as a grown man. "We're friends, Tink," I finally answer. "Friends with *secret* benefits."

"I won't hide anything from Spencer. I'm telling you that up front. I need someone to talk to about you."

I chuckle into the phone. "You talk about me?"

"Mostly we talk about your cock...sometimes how big of an asshole you are."

Now I'm full-on laughing. "Are you free tomorrow?"

"Tomorrow's Friday...I have work."

"Can I come take you to lunch?" Jesus, how fucking desperate am I to see this woman that I'm willing to drive two hours for a meal?

"Don't you uh...have a company to run or something?"

"Perks of being the boss...I work when I want, and tomorrow I want to take a friend to lunch."

There's a girlish giggle on the other end of the line and my heart leaps at the sound. "I can take a two-hour lunch from eleven to one. After that, I'll be working until seven or eight. Spence still isn't back from maternity leave, so it's just me."

"Perfect. I'll drop the girls off at their grandmother's house for the weekend, and I'll be on my way."

Gina gives me the address to her office, and we say our goodbyes. I fall asleep with a smile on my face for the first time in years. It feels good to have something to look forward to. Something for me.

"Tink?" I call out as I'm walking down the hall. "Your secretary said I could come on back."

"Hey, Jeff," she mutters without looking up from the chart she's writing in. It's a bit of a blow to my ego that she doesn't appear as excited to see me as I am her. "Do you wanna do this here or my place? I live about ten minutes away."

What the—? "Do what? You don't have restaurants in this little hick town?"

Her eyes finally meet mine. "Oh...You were serious 'bout lunch?"

"Uhh...yes?"

She shakes her head, rising from her seat and walks over to give me a hug. "Sorry, I thought that was code for a booty call." She rubs her manicured hands over my chest, straightening out my collar.

Tucking my finger beneath her chin, I tilt Gina's face up to mine. "I don't play games, Tink. When I want to fuck you, I will tell you that's what I want."

Her throat moves as she takes a big swallow. "Okay."

"Great. Grab your purse and point me to the nearest sit-down restaurant. Steak and potatoes sound good? Y'all have that 'round here?"

Boudreaux's is a floating restaurant. Like an enormous houseboat on the river. It's only a few minutes away from her office. Instantly I fall in love with the atmosphere. We cross over a long walking bridge from the parking lot to get onto the boat. My mouth salivates as I'm struck by an array of delicious aromas.

"Y'all follow me," our waitress Lucy instructs after grabbing two menus and napkin-wrapped silverware from beneath her podium.

"Lucy, can you seat us on the deck? Shade side, please?" Gina asks.

Our waitress nods, switching directions.

I follow behind Tink, admiring how good she looks all dolled up for work. Her navy dress is fitted, hugging all her curves. It ends at the knee with a small split in the back. She definitely handles those high heels better than I did. I laugh to myself. This is the first time I've seen her not dressed for the pool. Her long, blonde hair is curled in loose waves and she's wearing just enough makeup to accent her emerald eyes and pouty lips. She's stunning.

"This okay?" Lucy asks, stopping in front of the last table this side of the deck.

"Perfect. Thanks, Luce."

"No problem, honey. Y'all take a look at the menus and I'll be back shortly."

"This is a really nice place," I offer, looking around at the mossy oaks lining the water, the Cajun décor, and tapping my foot to the rhythm of Jolie Blonde. The air is hot, but the shade and fans keep it from being too sticky. I'm taken back to when I used to hang out drinking with my pops on his back patio. He loved his zydeco music. "I'm impressed."

Tink smiles. "I guess I should have asked if you were okay with eating outside. It's a little warm today, but this is my favorite spot."

"Nope. This is great," I say, opening my menu. "What's good here?"

"Thought you wanted steak and potatoes?"

"I did...but there's too much to choose from. Now, I can't decide."

"I like the stuffed, baked potato and crab cakes."

When our waitress returns I order the same as Gina, but with a side of fried catfish and crawfish étouffée.

"Where're you gonna put all that food?" Tink asks, laughing when the waitress walks off.

I lean back in my chair, patting my flat belly.

"I can't believe you really drove all this way for lunch."

"Totally worth it." I give her a wink. "Now, come dance with me." I offer her my hand when Wayne Toup's "Every Man Needs a Woman" starts to drift from the jukebox.

Gina's eyes bounce around nervously. "But, no one else is dancing."

"Don't make me go find another partner," I tease. "I bet that little old lady staring at us across the deck would be more than willing to dance with a handsome young fella." The woman catches me looking at her, so I wave, and she beams, waving back. "See?"

Shaking her head to herself, Tink rises from the chair,

placing her hand in mine. I lead her out just a few feet from our table, where there's a little more space, and pull her body against mine. After a few hesitant steps, she loosens up, and I can tell she's already forgotten that anyone else is here. Her heart beats fast against my chest as she rises up on her toes, curling her arms around my neck. My pulse begins to race.

There's only Tink and me and this moment, these lyrics weighing heavily between us. I sing the chorus into her ear about every man needing a woman and every woman a man, and her body melts into mine. I'm not sure what's happening between us. All I know is that this feels too damn good to let it go.

When the song ends, we walk quietly back to our table. I'm unsure of when things changed. When I stopped seeing her as merely an annoyance. When she became this constant thought running on loop through my head.

"You're looking at me funny, CEO."

"Sorry," I laugh. "Just got lost in my head for a minute."

"I hope you brought your appetites," Lucy says, arranging our plates on the table between us with the assistance of another server. "That's a whole lotta food for two tee-tiny people."

Chapter Twenty-Four

GINA

"You really managed to eat all that damn food," I laugh as Jeff groans in gluttonous misery. "I'd say I'm impressed, but I kinda wanna puke on your behalf."

Grinning, Jeffrey grabs the napkin out of his lap and begins dabbing at his mouth. "I may have to take a nap in my car before heading home." He stretches his arms above his head, offering me a glimpse at his happy trail as he arches back in his chair and yawns.

A feeling of dread washes over me at the thought of him leaving already. I mean, we haven't even gotten the chance to properly kiss. He can't just desert me like this—all sexually frustrated and tense. "The girls are with your parents, right?"

Jeff's finger traces the top of his water glass and he shakes his head. "Both of my parents died when Evangeline was a few years old." He gives me a tight-lipped smile. "They're with Jessica's mom. They go there every other weekend unless we

"Oh, gosh. I'm so sorry about your parents." *Open mouth. Insert foot.* You'd think as a freaking therapist I'd know to be careful of what I say to people. But this damn mouth... constantly getting me into trouble.

Jeffrey brushes it off. "It was a long time ago. They both died of cancer about a year apart. His face turns solemn. "After Mom went...Dad just kinda shut down. I've never known another man to be so in love with a woman." He smiles wistfully. "I think that's why I like this place so much. The music. The atmosphere. He'd have loved it."

"Cedar Grove is a great little town, full of character. But don't be fooled, everyone is all up in your business all the damn time. Drives me crazy."

"Ahh, that's with any small town, Tink. Livingston is just the same. Every place has its downfalls."

"I guess you're right. It's a tradeoff to be near friends and family."

We sit in companionable silence for a moment, staring out at the water. My insides are all jittery, still anticipating his looming departure. I'm a fucking cock fiend. There's no way I'm letting him go without getting my fix. "Hey...Why don't you go hang out at my place while I finish up work?" I offer, all nonchalant, but I'm literally on the verge of a panic attack. "I live right behind a little bar. I bet Spence could get her mom to go stay with the kids, and she and Coop could come out with us. Then they could finally meet you," I rush out without thinking. Do fuck buddies meet each other's friends? Heat floods my cheeks. "I mean, you know...if you don't have other plans."

Jeffrey smirks. "Is that—are you...*blushing*, Tink?" His hand reaches across the table, and he brushes the backs of his knuckles over my flaming skin. My scalp prickles, and I can feel the little baby hairs at the nape of my neck standing on end.

Ugh. "I haven't had an orgasm in two weeks," I whisper, leaning across the table. "I'm desperate."

His brows shoot up. "So, you want me to hang around just to fuck you?" He asks the question loudly, like he's trying to embarrass me, then laughs when I hide my face. "Is that all you want from me, Tink? Is that all I am to you? A slab of meat?"

"Shh. Lower your voice, asshole."

Jeff's arms cross on his chest. "Well?" He actually expects me to answer that?

Like a damn teenager, I feel all nervous and begin to develop a case of the jitters. "No...I think—I think I might actually like you, CEO." *Stupid.* I am so stupid. Who the hell admits that to their fuck buddy? I can't allow myself to be so vulnerable, so I add in a whisper, "But that dick don't hurt."

"Hear that everyone?" he shouts. "She likes me. She really likes me!" His finger lifts to wipe an imaginary tear from his eye, and I kinda wanna punch him.

"You're so embarrassing." Doesn't he know I have a reputation as a heartless bitch to uphold? Turning my face, I stare out at the lake, avoiding the stares and whispers of the other customers, most of whom I've known my entire life.

Jeff's foot brushes the side of my leg beneath the table, and I press my knees together. That little leg rub has me breaking out in goosies. "I'd be happy to stay and I'd love to meet your friends...I think."

"You think?"

"Just how much does your friend Spencer know about my cock?"

"Enough to pick it out in a lineup."

AFTER SHOWING JEFFREY HOW TO get to my apartment, he dropped me back at the office. Since then it's been nonstop clients. They're the only thing standing between me and my next orgasm. Well, that and a few hours at the bar, but that's all foreplay, and what girl doesn't love a little foreplay?

I can't stop staring at the clock. We were *just* together, and already my body yearns for his. This has honestly never happened to me before. And what's mind boggling is that it's not his cock I'm missing most. No, I know horny well...and this is so much more. It's just him. His presence. The way he looks at me. How my body feels electrified at his slightest touch. During the almost two hours I spent in his company today, I felt truly alive for the first time since...well, since the last time we were together.

When my last client finally departs, I rush back to my apartment to change. Spence and Coop are meeting us at nine, and that in itself has me all antsy. I've never needed her approval of any guy before, but for some reason I really want her to like Jeff.

"DAYUMMMM GINA!" JEFFREY HOWLS WHEN I step out into the living room after getting dressed for our night out. "Sorry," he says when I roll my eyes. "I've been dying to say that to you since we met. It finally works."

"Does it?"

Jeff rises from the couch and saunters over, grabbing my

hand and lifting it above my head. He gives me a little spin, ogling my outfit from every angle. It's a black strapless mini dress that hugs my body like a second skin. My hair is styled in a loose updo with tendrils framing my face. Fiery red pumps to match my lips complete the twenty-minute transformation. I'm confident in my appearance, but it feels good to know that he likes what he sees.

"You are so fucking sexy." Jeff slips both hands beneath the hair on either side of my face, loosely cupping my neck. His thumbs brush my chin, my jaw, my lips.

My breath hitches, and my heart's racing. I lean in, ready to finally feel the explosive connection of his lips on mine, but he pecks my cheek and backs away with a pained laugh. There's no way he can't see how stunned I am—how much I wanted that kiss.

His eyes do that sexy smolder thing he does so well. "Delayed gratification, Tink." He winks, then grabs his wallet, stuffing it into his back pocket, and jingles his car keys, as if to say, "Let's go." "Tonight," he grips my chin in his thumb and forefinger and breathes the one word promise against my eager lips.

"Just one kiss?" I practically beg. I'm desperate. Achy.

"Let's go." With his hand on the small of my back, he ushers us out of the door. "Your friends are going to be waiting on us."

"You're evil."

He looks my way, smirking as he turns the key, starting his truck. "Just imagine how good it's gonna be when we finally get each other alone tonight."

Jeff Ryan thinks he's being cute, but two can play at this game. Cock-tease is a sport I know very well.

Chapter Twenty-Five

JEFFREY

I drive literally two blocks, and we're already pulling into T-Boys, the little honkytonk-type bar near Gina's apartment complex. I use the term complex, loosely. There are maybe ten apartments total. It's quaint and quiet. I'm still unsure of how I feel about her living right behind a damn bar, though.

"This is it!" Tink unbuckles her seatbelt, opening the door and rushing out before I have the chance to even put the truck into park.

"I'd appreciate it if you'd at least give me the opportunity to be a gentleman," I admonish when I join her in the gravel lot.

Her hand rests on her hip. "What are you talking about?"

"I would've liked to open your door and help you down... hold your hand and escort you into the place...You know, like a real date."

"Jeffrey, we're fucking...exclusively. We're not dating."

Ouch. I feel my face fall and quickly school my features, hoping she can't see the disappointment.

"Dating involves feelings, Jeffrey, and that's exactly what we're trying to avoid, remember? You don't have to work to impress me. It's yours," she winks. "At least for now. Besides, I'm not used to boys doing that kind of thing anyway. I don't need it."

Are the men around here not brought up with respect? I was taught to always treat a woman like a lady. "I need it, Gina," I say, jabbing my thumb into my chest with each word. "When you're with me, I take care of you."

Her eyes widen, and she stares back at me in shock and maybe a little annoyance.

"I open the fucking doors."

"Oh...uh. Okay, CEO. If it makes you feel more like a man, I'll let you open my doors." She tilts her head to the side, batting her long lashes. "You wanna come get this one for me?" Her head tilts toward the wood door beneath the lopsided, hot pink neon sign flashing *T-Boys*. "Spence just texted, asking where we're at."

Nodding, I take a few steps, closing the space between us and lace my fingers in hers. "We're friends, Tink. That doesn't mean I can't treat you like a lady."

She snorts. "Well, you're the first to ever accuse me of being that."

After pulling the door opened, I grab her arm as she starts to walk in. "You're my lady, Tink."

"For now," she breathes into my ear before walking past me into the bar.

The entire place, inside and out, is made of cedar. From the walls to the bar to the floor. It gives it a nice, homey feel. Two pool tables sit in the center of the room, and there's a small stage in the far corner that looks like it doesn't get much use.

There are only a couple other people here. Two over at the pool tables, another fooling with the jukebox. The couple at the bar who are so engrossed with each other that they haven't noticed Gina standing right beside them must be Spencer and Cooper.

"Ahem," Tink clears her throat loudly to capture their attention.

"Gina. There you are!"

Tink's eyes rove over her bestie's body. "It's so nice to see you out of the house and dressed in something other than yoga pants. You look amazing."

The raven-haired beauty frowns. "Yeah, well, I feel like a fat ass." I remember how self-conscious Jess was after she had Evangeline. It took well over a year for her to feel good about herself again. For having just had twins, I think she looks amazing.

"You're beautiful," her husband says, squeezing her thigh beneath the bar. I turn my head as to not intrude upon their moment. "And so fucking sexy," he adds, nibbling on her ear.

"Josie!" Tink shouts, smacking her hand down on the bar a few times. "I need a cranberry and vodka." Then she looks up at me. "What're you having, Jeff?"

"I'll have a Bud Light."

"And a Bud Light!" That girl has got a set of pipes on her for sure.

"Thanks, Tink." It's a little weird having a girl order for me, but I decide to keep that thought to myself. Doors first…one step at a time.

"I'm Cooper, Spencer's husband." He reaches his hand out. "I'm sure you've heard a lot about her."

"Jeff," I answer, shaking his hand. "Yeah, from what I gather these two are thick as thieves."

Coop chokes on his beer. "Ya got that right. And just as fucking sneaky." He turns to look at the girls, who are already deep in conversation. There's a great deal of pride and admiration in his face. "You gotta watch those two, man. Two for the price of one...You piss one off, you deal with both. Always remember that."

"Remember what?" his wife, Spencer asks, sticking her hand out for mine. "I'm Spence, nice to meet you Jeff. I've heard *good* things." Her brows waggle and I know she's referring to the size of my dick. This could be the most awkward introduction of my life.

"I was just telling him how you and Gina are a packaged deal," he answers, smiling lovingly at his wife.

Spencer beams. "Double the fun."

"Yeah...I was thinking more along the lines of double the trouble."

"Well, who's your good lookin' friend, Gina?" the bartender asks, leaning over with her forearms resting on the top of the bar, displaying a hefty helping of cleavage.

"Back off, Josie," Spencer warns. "He's with Gina."

Josie, a pretty little blonde with next to no clothes, cowgirl boots, and a smile as sweet as iced tea, laughs. "Please. Everybody knows, ain't nobody *with* Gina...well, not longer than for a night or two anyhow."

"Well," I drawl, interrupting their conversation. "I plan to be *with* Tink for as long as she'll put up with me." With an arm around her bare shoulders, I pull her close. She surprises me by wrapping an arm around my waist and grabbing a handful of my ass. I never know what to expect with her.

"Well, you've got a lot,"—her eyes drop to my crotch— "working in your favor, CEO."

"Oooooh, girl...I thought you didn't fall in love?" Josie presses. "Looks like you got it bad."

"She's not *in love*," Spence answers in a mocking tone. "The girl done went and got dickstruck."

Every last drop of blood in my body rushes to my face. "Thanks, Gina," I mutter.

"Remember fart girl?" She purses her lips, narrowing her eyes at me. "Payback's a motherfucker. Remember that. I will *always* get mine."

"Wait?" Coop says, holding his hand up. "Who's fart girl?"

"Don't you dare," my little vixen warns, shooting me daggers.

After a few drinks and some small talk, Josie comes up with the incredibly stupid idea of playing the dating game.

"Come on, y'all," she slurs. "It's gonna be fun."

"But we're married," Coop argues. "Not dating."

"Yeah, and we're just fucking," I say, motioning between Tink and myself.

"Jeez, CEO. You make us sound so cheap," my tipsy fuckbuddy whines.

I pull her into my lap, nibbling on her ear. "But, it's really good. Really high-quality fucking."

"Damn straight it is."

"All right. Deep-V Diver," Josie says, eyeing me with a grin. "And you too, Coop. Go pick a few songs on the jukebox and don't come back 'til I holler for ya."

Begrudgingly Cooper and I walk to the other end of the bar. "This is going to be so bad," he grumbles. "Hope you're prepared to sleep on the sofa."

"Maybe for you," I snicker. "You're married. You have to know everything. Tink and I are just getting to know each other."

There's a long silence while we each take a turn filling the jukebox queue.

"Be careful with her, Jeffrey," Coop warns out of the blue. I get the feeling he's been waiting to get me alone and has finally decided to take his shot while he's got it. "Lord knows I am not the one to give dating advice. I lost fifteen years with Spence before getting her back, due to my own stupidity." He shakes his head in disgust. "Just know Gina's not as tough as she seems."

"I'll do my best," I assure him, impressed by the fact that he stood up for her. I'm glad she has friends like Cooper and Spencer in her life.

"Boys! Come on back," Josie shouts, waving at us with both hands in the air.

I start to head back for the bar when I feel a hand clamp my shoulder. "Do better than try, CEO."

Chapter Twenty-Six

GINA

"Ready, boys?" Josie asks the men when the men return to their stools at the bar, looking like they're headed for war. They are so ridiculous.

Both of them answer at the same time. "No." It takes all of my strength not to laugh at how green in the face they both are. What the hell do they think's gonna happen?

"So, I asked the ladies here what their favorite thing was about each of you," Josie says, pulling her clipboard out from beneath the counter. "Cooper, you can go first."

"Shit," Coop groans, knowing full well how competitive Spencer is. "Did she go funny or serious with the answers?"

Josie wags her finger at him. "Can't tell you that. Just answer the way you think your wife would have answered."

He worries his lip, giving the question a lot of thought. Really, the answer is so damn obvious. "Ummm. I think Spencer's favorite thing about me is...my...hair?" Or, not...

"Your *hair*, Cooper? Really?" Spencer gives him the cold shoulder and a look of disgust.

"BAMP!" Josie shouts. "Wrong answer. Spencer said her favorite thing about Coop was what an amazing father he is to their five children."

"Awwww," Josie and I chime together as Spencer glares at her husband out of the corner of her eye.

"Jeffrey, I asked Gina here the same question."

"That's easy," he says grinning ear to ear. "My cock." He blurts out that answer without reservation. Have I mentioned how much better I like his stuffy ass drunk?

"Ding! Ding! Ding!" Josie chimes. "One point for team Fuck Buddies."

Jeff and I slap each other double high-fives.

"Get your shit together, Cooper Hebert," my drunk best friend warns her husband.

Josie pops the caps off two beer bottles and sets them on the bar in front of the men before continuing. "Question number two. I asked the girls if they thought you'd rather go swimming with ducks or turtles."

Cooper smiles big, ready to redeem himself. There's no way he'll miss it. Sea turtles are Spencer's favorite. "Turtles."

"Yes!" Spencer shouts, wrapping her arms around her husband's neck. "You're amazing. I love you so much."

And...now her tongue is down his throat. *Bipolar much?*

"Beaver Basher?" Josie chuckles, looking to Jeffrey. "Same question." He may just club me to death with that big dick by the time this night is over if Josie doesn't cut it out.

I suck in my lips, trying my best to hide a smile. He's going to fucking hate me when he hears my answer.

His head drops into his hand, shaking side to side as he tugs his blond locks. "Dolphins." Jeff looks over and glares my way. "There's no way she gave any answer other than dolphins."

Josie's mouth falls open in shock. She was so sure he wouldn't get it since my answer wasn't even a choice. But I was willing to get it wrong just to see the look on his face.

"Such bullshit," my moody best friend growls, slamming her fist down on the bar.

"That's one point each for teams Wedded Bliss and Fuck Buddies. Fuck Buddies are up by one. The final question asked was, what do they think is your greatest fear?" She looks to Cooper for his answer.

"Losing you again," Coop says, to his wife, without needing a single second to think it over. Spence nods, her eyes welling with tears, and smashes her lips against his.

"Alrighty then." Josie looks pointedly at the married couple eating each others' faces then back to us. "Jeff?"

He sets his beer down on the cocktail napkin in front of him and gets this vacant look in his shimmering blue eyes. "Not being the father my wife would have wanted for my girls." His voice cracks, and he clears his throat. His Adam's apple bobs with a hard swallow.

Josie, Spencer, and my eyes all fill with tears at the sight of this broken man. It suddenly feels like I'm drowning in a pool of water, the thickness of the moment suffocating me.

"She answered, 'disappointing your children.'" Josie's voice is heavy with emotion. "She didn't mention your wife. I'm sorry." Her apology is obviously for more than just missing a question in this stupid game. "I'm going to have to mark that as a no and call a draw...Be right back." Josie rushes off to the little office behind the bar dabbing at her tears with a napkin.

After composing herself, our favorite bartender returns with shots of Fireball on the house. "For being such good sports." She sets two in front of each of us, and we toss them back immediately, but in no way does it feel like a celebration.

"Thanks, Josie."

"Dance with me." I grab hold of Jeffrey's hand and gently pull. He's been a little off since that last question. Hell, we all have. I'm desperate to feel close to him again. I'm trying to be understanding and not to let it get to me when he brings Jessica up. I know he's hurting, and I hate that I sometimes feel jealousy over a woman who did nothing wrong. It's just hard when I constantly feel like I'm competing with her ghost. But, competing for what, exactly? Jeff and I are friends. *Just friends.* And I want him to feel comfortable talking to me, even if it's about her. No matter how much this hurts, it can't even compare with the pain he must feel in his heart.

"Sure, yeah." His smile feels strained, and it makes my heart lurch. There's a heaviness hanging in the air between us. I hate it.

When we reach the dance floor, I slide my hands up his chest slowly, lacing my fingers behind his neck. His heart is like a jackhammer pounding against his chest, hard and fast. The beginning chords to *Give Me Love* by Ed Sheeran drift from the speakers. Of all songs...why this one? In the very first line he asks the girl to give him "love like her." And it hits so close to home that I find myself trembling in Jeffrey's arms. My throat swells, feeling tight, and my lips begin to quiver. *Stop it, Gina. Stop it, now.* But I can't stop the tears from building in my eyes. From rolling down my cheeks.

He pulls me tighter, dropping his lips to my neck and feathering light kisses along the sensitive skin, setting my blood on fire. Our bodies move so perfectly in tune to the music. To each other. "I'm sorry, Tink," he whispers against my ear.

"I'm fine," I lie, burying my face into his shoulder.

"I'm hurting you."

Shaking my head, I pull back so that he can see my face, so he believes that I mean what I'm about to say. "You didn't." My head shakes. "You didn't hurt me, Jeffrey. I had a little too much to drink, and I'm feeling overly emotional. I'm sad *for* you. Not because of you."

He stares into my eyes, searching for the truth, and I don't know whether or not he can see through the lie I want to believe so badly, but his hand grips my chin and his mouth molds to mine. His kiss is slow and sure and feels more intimate than any other we've shared. He's making love to my mouth, apologizing to me in the language in which we communicate best. My knees grow weak, and my heart begins to race. I'm not even sure how many songs we spend out on that dance floor, healing our broken hearts, but at some point Spencer is there tapping me on the shoulder.

"Hey, babe. Sorry to interrupt. Coop and I are gonna head home, and I didn't want to leave without saying goodbye." She sighs deeply. "I'm exhausted."

Pulling my lips from Jeff's, I swipe the back of my hand over my mouth. "Gosh, I'm sorry Spence. I'm ignoring you."

"Girl. Shut up. Do not even go there. We see each other all the time." Her attention diverts to my date. "I had a great time, and it was so nice to meet you, Jeffrey."

The flush of embarrassment at being interrupted that erupts on Jeff's cheeks is the cutest fucking thing I've ever seen. "Thanks, Spencer. It was really nice meeting you both as well."

"You ready to head home—uh, I mean, back to my place?" I ask once Spence and Coop are gone.

"I thought you'd never ask."

The two-minute drive to my apartment is made in complete

silence until he pulls into the spot beside my Audi, and I move to open the door.

"Don't." He gives me what I presume are his daddy eyes, dark and ominous.

My hand jerks back from the handle, an automatic response to his authoritative tone. Normally, I'd tell a guy to fuck right off for ordering me around, but when Jeff does it, butterflies flutter in my tummy.

I watch as he exits the vehicle and walks around to my side. The door opens, but instead of offering me his hand like I'm expecting, he slips one arm through my bent knees and scoops me up, cradling my body against his hard chest, causing me to yelp in surprise.

"I've been waiting all night for this, Tink," Jeffrey rasps, staring deep into my eyes, bringing my vaginal heartbeat back with a vengeance. Then his lips seize mine as he starts for the apartment, kicking the truck door shut with his foot. Little moans and grunts escape from the back of his throat and send a jolt right between my legs. I fucking love the noises he makes.

When we reach the door, he finally sets me to my feet, strumming his fingers on the frame with impatience as I fish through my purse for the keys and unlock the apartment.

"Do you want anything to eat or drink?" My voice shakes with need as I set my purse and keys down on the little console table at the entrance.

"No." He untucks his black button down from his jeans and slips out of his shoes. "I just need you, Tink." That broken look from earlier is back. I want to be his relief. I don't care if he's just using me. I will martyr myself if it eases even an ounce of the heartache reflected in those baby blues.

"You have me, Jeff," I breathe against his lips, and his tongue darts out, licking the seam of my mouth. "Take me."

His hands grip the backs of my thighs, just below the hem of my dress, and he lifts me off the floor. I wrap my legs around his waist and my hands grip two fistfuls of his hair, as he starts for the bedroom, his lips never abandoning mine.

When he sets me down on the edge of the bed, I attack his belt and button, pulling out his already hard cock and bringing it to my lips. I'm so consumed with the need to make him feel good that my own relief is no longer at the forefront of my priorities.

"No, Tink." Jeff steps back, and his dick juts straight out, beckoning me.

Sigh. Not this again. "I swear I'm good at it. It was just the boat, I was si—"

Jeffrey reaches down, cupping my chin in his hand. His thumb rolls over my bottom lip. "Come here," he says, guiding me to standing. When I start to speak, he shakes his head, resting a finger against my lips to silence me. Biting back a smirk, he takes me by complete surprise. "Tonight is all about you, *my lady.* I'm going to worship this body," he says, as his hungry eyes drink me in like a fine wine, "the way a *real* man should."

Liquid desire swirls in my belly at the promise in his words. Suddenly I'm feeling like an inexperienced girl, despite the dozens of sexual partners I've had. Molten fire shoots through my veins when he brings his lips to my collarbone, kissing and flitting his expert tongue along the bend of my neck while reaching around and lowering the zipper on my dress.

Jeff hisses his appreciation as the black fabric slips down my body, pooling at my feet. One of his hands sneaks around to my back, flicking the clasp of my strapless bra, leaving me standing in nothing but a pair of red heels and black lace panties.

Sucking in a breath, he shakes his head as if in disbelief. "So beautiful." His hand grips my chin, and he pulls my lips to his, sliding his mouth over mine and stealing my breath away.

The backs of his knuckles brush over my nipples, damn near causing me to come unglued. "Jeffrey, please," I beg.

"Get in the bed," he orders while removing the rest of his clothes. He climbs in over me, resting his forearms on either side of my head, his hard body pressed to mine. For a long moment he doesn't breathe a word, just stares down at me.

"Kiss me, Jeffrey," I finally whisper when I can't take it anymore. Every fiber of my being is bursting for release while we lay here still as statues. My hands reach up to brush the hair from his forehead and trace the line of his jaw. "Kiss me before I go crazy."

Leisurely his mouth lowers to join mine. A soft press of his lips. A light flick of his tongue. Torturously slow, he tastes every inch of my body, working his way down my neck and trailing his velvety tongue down my breastbone. He nips and sucks at my stiff nipples, all the while holding my hands by my sides. When he reaches my inner thighs, my back arches from the bed. Then his tongue trails along my slit, swirling around my clit, and I swear I can see the fucking stars. He brings me to the brink, backing off just when I'm about to explode.

"J—Jeffrey, please. I need you. N—now!" Within seconds he's hovering over me, pushing inside of me, making love to my mouth while he rocks in and out as if we have all the time in the world. As if he's savoring every sacred moment.

Finally, he releases his hold on my hands and I reach between us, massaging my clit and pulling his hair. Jeff's thrusts become harder and faster, matching the rhythm of my frantic movements. It isn't long before my tsunami of desire crests, and his body tenses with mine and we both cry out, finding our release together.

Chapter Twenty-Seven

GINA

"Hello?"

"Hey, Tink. Can you, uh...You think you could come over?"

What? "Right now?"

"Please?"

"It's Wednesday, CEO. I'm at work...I have to work tomorrow. And anyway, aren't the girls home?"

We've been together every other weekend for the past few months, meeting up when the girls go to their grandmother's house at either his place or mine. I have yet to see Willow or Evangeline since the cruise. They have no clue we're seeing each other and he was adamant it stay that way. So, him begging me to come over in the middle of the week is taking me completely off guard.

"Evangeline got her period," he finally explains, sounding completely at a loss for what to do.

"Oh..."

"She's locked in her room and won't stop crying. It's the

second day of school and everyone saw...It was all over her pants."

"Oh, God, that poor baby."

"Gina?"

"Yeah?" I ask, trying to figure out how the heck I'm going to leave in the middle of the work day to drive out there.

"I don't have anyone else. I—I didn't know who to call."

"I'm on my way."

Two hours later, I'm climbing the familiar stone steps, about to knock on Jeff's front door. This roiling acidic feeling in my gut, however, is new. I'm not sure he's thought this through or what he plans to tell his kids about why the woman he could barely tolerate on the cruise is suddenly showing up on their doorstep.

Ah, well, guess I'm about to find out. Taking a deep breath, I press my finger to the doorbell and wait.

"Oh, thank God," Jeff says, swinging the door open and ushering me inside. "Thank you so much for coming."

"No problem." I clear my throat, trying to disguise the hurt in my voice. No hug. No kiss. Not even a fucking handshake or a pat on the back. I knew not to expect the affection I've come to crave from this man with the girls around, but that doesn't mean it doesn't still sting.

"Gigi!" Willow screams, running at me from the living room. The sight of those little pig tails bouncing tugs on my heart. I've missed her more than I even realized. "What you doin' here?"

"Hey, baby girl." Swinging her up into my arms, I hold her

close, giving her a good, tight squeeze. "I've missed you."

"I misseded you too. Did you bring Tyle?"

"No. Not this time. I'm sorry. I came to see about Vangie. Your daddy told me she's having a rough day."

Willow huffs a long and drawn out breath. "Her's in her room bein' dratic."

Furrowing my brow, I look to Jeff for clarification.

"Dramatic."

Ahh. "Got it…So, what exactly do you need me to do?"

Jeff shrugs. The poor man looks so defeated. "I guess just try to calm her down and teach her how to handle all of that."

"You *did* get her feminine products, right?"

"Of course," he says shaking his head at me. "I did have a wife, you know."

"Just checking."

"I picked her up from school and dropped her off at home, so she could get in the tub. Then, I went to the grocery store and grabbed her literally one of everything. Probably even two of some. I just threw a bunch of things into the cart. She's got bags of shit to choose from, Tink."

Pulling in my lips, I hold back a laugh. "Great. Okay, well…I'm goin' in. Wish me luck."

Tap. Tap. Tap.

"Leave me alone, Dad. I'm not going back there. Ever!"

Yikes. "Hey, Evangeline, it's me, uhh Gina. Can I come in?"

"Gina?" she questions from right on the other side of the door. "What are you doing here?"

"Your dad thought maybe you needed a woman to talk to…"

I lean my head against the door, listening to her sniffling.

After a long pause, the lock clicks and it slowly starts to swing open. "Oh, honey," I say when I get a look at her red, swollen face. "Come here."

Evangeline falls into my arms sobbing. "It wa—was awful, Gina." Her little body shakes and my heart twists into knots, as I smooth down the hair at the back of her head.

After about a minute she moves to sit on the edge of her bed, patting for me to sit beside her. "One of the football players tapped me on the shoulder as I was leaving class and told me." Huge sobs wrack her tiny frame. "A football player! My life is over."

"Evangeline." I wait for her to calm down and look at me. "Today sucked," I agree. "But I promise this is not the end of the world. Even though I know it must feel like it right now."

She snorts. "Maybe not for you."

"I'm not going to downplay your embarrassment, Vangie. It will be rough for a few days and then everyone who saw will forget, and it'll all blow over. And who knows? Maybe that boy was the only one to see and is enough of a gentleman to keep his mouth shut."

"Maybe," she agrees, but doesn't look at all convinced.

My eyes well up as I look at this little girl becoming a woman without a mother to show her the way. Mine was a piece of work, but she had me loaded down with hygiene products in my backpack from the age of eight. As soon as my first period finished, that woman had me at the doctor's office for birth control. Just what every eleven-year-old girl needs. "Vangie," I say, giving her hand a little squeeze. "You're becoming a woman."

She snorts, laughing through her tears. "That's such a cliché thing to say, Gina."

"But it's true, and I know it's scary and disgusting, but it's also a rite of passage. We *all* go through it, baby. You are not alone. The important thing now is to make sure you're prepared not only to deal with the mess, but with all of the other changes that go along with it."

"I know." Vangie waves me off. "I know all about how babies are made. They taught us that in like fifth grade."

"Good," I say breathing a sigh of relief. "But there's more."

"Yippee!"

"First things first," I say, slapping my hands together. "Show me the supplies your father picked up."

After sorting through the bags, we determine she has enough pads and tampons to last her through an apocalypse. I explain to her about trying out the different sizes and seeing which ones feel most comfortable, but also control her flow. I explain about Toxic Shock Syndrome and the importance of changing her tampon at least every eight hours.

"Yeah, I don't think I'll be using those anymore. I tried one earlier and it hurt so bad."

Well, that doesn't sound right at all. "The tampon hurt to put in? You shouldn't really feel it once it's inside."

Evangeline laughs. "That's what the instructions said too, but that plastic hurts. Maybe the one I wore was too big?"

"The plastic?" Oh, God. "You mean the applicator?"

"I guess."

This time I can't help but to laugh. "You left it in?"

"Uh...yeah. I did what the instructions said. I put it up in there and pulled the skinny piece out and threw it away...Why are you laughing? Did I do something wrong?"

"Give me a damn tampon," I say, snatching a box from the

side of her. "Okay. Pretend my hand is the opening to a vagina, okay?" I ask, making a loose fist, so I can insert the tampon into the hole. "Okay, so you take off the wrapper and stick the fat part up inside."

"I did that."

"Okay, so this is the step you missed. Pay attention. After you stick it in, you have to push the skinny tube into the big one...Oh, but make sure you're still holding the big one too."

Vangie's eyes grow big.

"It sounds a lot more difficult than it really is. We'll practice a few times before you try it again. Anyway, so you push this little tube, and that will force the cotton wad, which is the part that is supposed to stay in there, up higher into your vagina. Then you pull *both* pieces of the plastic applicator out and are left with a string which will hang an inch or two out of your opening...When you go to the bathroom to change it, you just pull the string, and it comes right out."

After practicing a few times in her hand, Vangie ventures to the bathroom for another attempt. When she comes out smiling, I know she's one step closer to being able to deal with all of this.

"All right, let's go."

"Go?" she asks looking around her sanctuary. "Where're we going?"

"To the store. We need face wash for pimples, Midol for cramps, and a little pocket calendar to keep track of your schedule. And ice cream, Evangeline. We're gonna go eat our feelings. How's that sound?"

Evangeline's face lights up. "Thank you, Gina."

"Anytime, sweetie."

Chapter Twenty-Eight

JEFFREY

After nearly two hours have gone by, Tink finally comes strolling down the stairs wearing the world's strongest poker face. I can't read her expression at all. "Well?" I ask, when she brushes past me to sit on the sofa. "How'd it go?"

"Fine." She crosses one leg over the other, looking down into her lap and fooling with her nails.

"That's it?"

"I'm ready," Vangie calls, descending the stairs before I can get anything else out of Gina. She's in jeans and a dressy top, her hair in a bun, and ballet flats. *And*, she's smiling. Thank the Lord.

"Ready?" I look from Evangeline to Gina, who is now up from the sofa and digging her keys out of her purse. "What are we ready for?"

"We're," Tink stresses, motioning from herself to Evangeline, "going to the store to pick up a few more things she's going to need and..." She looks around the room before whispering, "Out for ice cream," into my ear. "I'll bring something back for you and little bit...I'd take her, but I kinda think this is a big deal for Evangeline and wanna make it all about her."

"Of course," I say, impressed by her thoughtfulness. Not that she isn't thoughtful, just well, she doesn't have kids, and that she has the foresight to realize having Willow around might bother Evangeline is endearing me to her even more. "All right, well, you two have fun," I say, reaching into my back pocket for my wallet. I try handing Gina some money, but she shoves it away, looking insulted.

"I got it, Daddy big bucks." Gina's tongue pokes out, and she scrunches up her nose. "Let me do this for her." Then our eyes lock in an intense stare, and she adds in a voice just above a whisper, "Let me do this for *you*."

"Bye, Dad." Evangeline rushes over, lifting up to her toes, and plants a kiss on my cheek. "Thanks for calling Gina."

"No problem, sweet pea. I'm glad she was able to help."

"We shouldn't be more than an hour or three," Tink calls back, as I watch my girls head for the door.

Evangeline walks out ahead of her and Gina pokes her head back in, blowing me a kiss.

On instinct my hand lifts to catch it, just like I would for Willow. But instead of putting it in my pocket, I rub it on my crotch, smirking at Tink.

"Tease." She lurks in the doorway a moment longer, undressing me with her eyes. *God, I want her so fucking bad.*

I clear my throat to break the trance. "Willow and I will cook dinner while you're out."

"Oh, am I staying for dinner?"

"Yeah." I nod, swallowing down a lump of emotion. "I think you are."

Her hand flattens out, and she lifts it to her head giving me a military salute. "See you then."

"Go count out four forks from the drawer and set one next to each plate," I instruct my little helper, as I finish mixing the mashed potatoes.

"I'm so cited, Daddy! Is Gigi gonna sweep here?"

I wish. "No, baby. She just came to see about your sister. Gina has to work tomorrow morning."

"Dey here!" Willow screams. The forks clang on the tile as she drops them and takes off running for the foyer.

The front door swings open and Evangeline and Gina burst through in a fit of giggles. I can't even express what it does to my heart to see such a drastic transformation in my little girl from earlier today.

"What you dot me?" Willow asks, tugging on the bottom of Gina's shirt.

"Well," she says, pulling a bag from behind her back. "There might be something in this one for you."

Willow snatches it right out of her hand. "Shokins!" she shouts, jumping up and down. "Tank you, Gigi!"

"You're very welcome, princess. We brought you and Daddy back some ice cream too, but that's going to go in the freezer 'til after dinner, okay?"

Willow nods, fighting to tear open the package of rubber grocery toys. I'll never understand their appeal, but she loves the damn things. They're the little girl version of Legos, only softer. You'll find them in every nook and cranny of this house.

Every fiber of my being is dying to give Gina a proper welcome back—to take her in my arms and taste those full, pouty lips. But I can't do that with the girls around. I want her to the point it's becoming almost painful. So, I remain in the kitchen, a safe distance away. "Dinner's ready!" I shout from the doorway, and like a herd of starving buffalo, they race for the kitchen.

Gina and I sit across from each other at our little four-seater table and I make a concerted effort not to sit here and stare at her while she eats. She lifts the first bite of steak into her mouth and moans her approval. My dick jumps to attention. It's a sound he knows well.

Discreetly, I sneak my hand beneath the table, shifting my dick to a more comfortable position. When I look up, Gina winks, giving me a knowing smile.

"Did you girls find everything you needed?" I ask, trying to distract myself.

"Mmmhmm," Evangeline answers, while chewing her food. "And Gina gave me her number in case I need to talk to her about any girl stuff."

Tink's face flushes, and she worries her lower lip between her teeth. "I hope that was okay...I guess I should have asked first."

"It's perfectly fine. I appreciate everything you've done for Vangie today, Gina. This is so far out of my element it isn't even funny."

"You know I adore your girls. It's been my pleasure."

By the time we've finished eating, it's after bedtime. All the excitement of today put us behind schedule.

"Will you stay until after I've tucked them in?" I ask,

desperate for a moment alone with my lady before she leaves.

Tink nods, plopping herself on the sofa with the remote and shoos me away. "I'll be right here. But I can only stay a few minutes. I have a long drive back."

The girls both kiss Gina goodnight without even being asked, and I'm forced to look away. I knew they'd bonded on the cruise, but seeing them together again and that their connection has only intensified...It has me wishing for things I know I can't have. Conflicting emotions war in my head and in my heart. How can this feel so right and so fucking wrong all at once?

"That was quick," Tink says, sitting up and stretching her arms above her head as she releases a big yawn.

"That was only round one," I laugh, shaking my head. "Willow will be down at least three more times for water, kisses, and to pee, even though she just did all three."

"Aren't kids awesome?" Tink laughs, toeing her shoes back on. I hate that she has to leave. But I know I can't ask her to stay.

I nod. "Somethin' like that..." When she rises from the couch, I take her hand in mine, to halt her movement for the door. "Thank you for today, Tink. I know it was wrong of me to ask this of you. I had no right—"

"Hey? We're friends, right?" she asks, squeezing my fingers in her tiny hand.

"Yeah."

"Friends are there for each other, Jeff. It means a lot that you trusted me to be here for you." She swallows audibly. "And even more that you trusted me enough to be here for her."

My throat starts to swell. "Come sit with me on the porch for a minute, Tink?" I can't bear to let her go already.

She nods, following me through the house to the screened-in porch out back where the two of us have spent many nights together just talking and fooling around.

We sit side by side on the white wicker swing. I wrap my arm around her shoulders, pulling her close, and it feels like I can truly breathe for the first time today. "This is nice."

Her head bobs against my chest, and she sniffs.

"You okay, Tink?"

"Mmhmm," she says, wrapping her arms around my waist and holding me in a vice grip.

"You sure?" I ask, lifting her chin, effectively forcing her to look up so I can see her face. "Why are you crying, babe?"

"Gah." She releases her arms, sitting up straight to swipe beneath her eyes. "Fucking horny tears," she growls, and I let it go, because we're friends, and this feels like dangerous territory. And because even if she's falling for me, the way I think I'm probably already gone for her, I don't want to acknowledge it. *Ever.* Because then I'll have to end this, and I'm not ready to let go. I'm beginning to think I may never be.

Chapter Twenty-Nine

GINA

"Okay, you've already admitted that your anger is one of the biggest issues in your marriage, right? So, if this marriage means as much as you say it does, then what steps can you take to better control that anger, Mr. Giles?"

I'm only half paying attention as he spouts off all the techniques we've been discussing during his sessions, when my phone buzzes in my lap. With a quick glance, I see that it's Evangeline. And now it's even harder to pay attention, but I resist the urge to check my phone and push through the last fifteen minutes of his session. He is paying for my services after all.

"Mr. Giles," I hold out my hand for his. "I'd like you to contact the guy on that card I gave you for anger management. I'm afraid if you can't get this under control...Well, I don't need to tell you what that'll mean, or you wouldn't be here in the first place."

"Yes, ma'am. I'm desperate. I'll give him a call as soon as I get out of here."

"Very good." I nod, ready to shove him out the door. "I'll see you next week."

When my office is finally empty, I collapse into my chair and pull up my message from Evangeline.

Evangeline: Hey, Gina. Do you have time to talk? I think something's wrong.

It's Friday. Just two days since the whole period debacle and I've been thinking of her nonstop but didn't want to be the first to message. Somehow, I'm scared I'll overstep. Even if Jeff did give us his blessing. His kids are slippery territory, and I don't want to do anything to screw this up.

Me: I'm between clients now. Can you talk?

Evangeline: Yeah, I just got home. Dad's still at work.

Reaching across my desk I buzz Lois, my receptionist.
"Yes, Gina?"

"Can you hold my next client up front for a few minutes? I need to make an important call. I'll buzz you back when I'm ready."

"Sure thing."

"Thanks."

After resting my desk phone back in its cradle, I dial Vangie on my cell.

"Hello," she moans, sounding like death.

"What's wrong, baby?" Instantly my pulse starts racing.

It takes her a moment to stop crying enough to talk. "It just hurts so bad. My head and my—my stomach."

"I know, honey. Did you try the Midol we picked up the other day?"

She whimpers. "Yeah, but I can't take it again for another hour."

"Listen," I say, now pacing my office. "Plug in that heating pad and lay down with it across your abdomen for a while. This seems a bit excessive. I'm going to talk to your dad about taking you to a gynecologist. Just to check and make sure everything's okay. Sometimes they can put you on birth control, and it helps immensely."

"Oh, God. There's no way I could ask him to put me on birth control. Dad would flip his shit."

That makes me laugh, because she is absolutely right. "That's why I'll talk to him. Go get some rest, and I'll check on you after work."

"Thanks, Gigi," she groans, ending the call.

My last two clients' sessions fly by, and I'm off by five. It's so nice having Spence back in the office and getting out before dark. Those long nights were really wearing on me.

As soon as I'm in my car, I text Vangie to see how she's feeling, getting no response. I don't want to call and bother her if she's sleeping, so I decide I'll try her again later.

When I get home, I text again. And once again there's no response, so I call Jeffrey.

"Hey, gorgeous, I was just about to call you," he answers. His cheery tone brings a smile to my face.

"Were you?" I ask, popping a frozen dinner into the microwave.

"I miss you," he mumbles into the phone, indicating Willow must be nearby.

"You just saw me day before yesterday," I tease, although I miss him so much my insides are twisted up into knots. The girls are staying home this weekend which means I won't see him for a whole week. My plan is to spend as much time as I can with Spence and the kids to try to keep my mind off my *not boyfriend*. I really suck at this fuck buddy thing.

He chuckles. "So?"

"Hey, how's Vangie?" I ask, changing the subject. "She wasn't feeling well earlier, and I texted a few times to check in, but she's not answering."

"I just came down from her room. She's in bed with the heating pad, passed out."

"Poor baby."

"Come over?" he blurts out of nowhere. "Spend the night...I'll take the couch, and you can have my bed."

Now my heart is racing for an entirely different reason. Lines are blurring, but I don't have enough self-preservation to say no, so instead I ask, "Are you sure?"

"The girls will love it, and then you can check on Vangie yourself," he adds. "Perfect excuse."

"Jeffrey...What are you going to do when Evangeline eventually asks about us? She's not a little kid. She's going to realize something's going on. Women don't just drive two hours to sleep at a guy friend's house."

"Sure, they do." The man is completely deluded. "I'll tell her we're just friends, and you enjoy spending time with them. They don't need to know more than that."

I'd be lying if I said it didn't hurt to be treated like his dirty little secret, but I knew exactly what I was getting myself into and dove in head first. I have no right to feel the way I do.

"I should say no." With the phone resting between my chin and shoulder, I retrieve my Banquet spaghetti and meatballs from the microwave, tossing the little tray to the counter.

"What time can you be here?"

"See you at seven."

"Gigi, you tame back!"

Jeff smiles down at me, grabbing the overnight bag from my hand so I can properly greet my little friend. Before he heads toward his bedroom with my things, he gives me a sexy wink.

"Hey, baby girl." I swoop her up into my arms like a little baby and fall into the plush, oversized armchair, snuggling her to my chest. "I didn't get to spend enough time with you the other day. I had to come back and get my little girl fix."

"Gina?" Evangeline groans, rubbing sleep from her eyes as she steps into the room. "What are you doing here?"

"Hey, honey." I pat the space next to me. "I was worried, and asked your father if I could come back and check on you. How're you feeling?"

Vangie curls into my side, resting her head on my shoulder, "A little better, I think."

With my right hand, I smooth the hair from her face, pressing a kiss to her forehead.

"I'm glad you're here," she says, yawning.

"So am I, sweet girl."

"Gigi, wake up!"

My eyes flutter open to find Willow bouncing in Jeff's bed next to me and Evangeline carrying a tray of bacon and eggs. "Made you breakfast," that little angel says, smiling sweetly.

My eyes feel wet again. And this time I can't blame it on my vagina, because Jeff is nowhere around. Dammit. "Thank you, Vangie. That's so sweet."

She shrugs her shoulders as if it's nothing, setting the tray next to me and swooping her little sister up before she can dump the food all over the bed. "This little monkey helped."

"Yeah," Willow agrees, struggling to get out of her sister's arms. "I putted the jelly on your toast."

That explains the gobs of grape jam. I couldn't wipe the smile from my face if I tried. "Thank you both so much."

"You're welcome. Enjoy."

When the two girls exit the room, shutting the door behind them, I allow the tears to fall. I feel like I'm living someone else's life. Then I remember that I am and that none of this is mine, and I cry some more. *What the hell is happening to me?*

Time to call in reinforcements.

"Hey, hooch."

"Quick," I say sniveling into the phone. "Make me laugh."

"Are you—What the hell did he do to you?" Spencer shouts, jumping to the wrong conclusion.

"It wasn't him," I rush out. "It was the girls."

Spence groans. "Oh, God. What happened?"

"They m—made me b—breakfast," I sob, and my best friend loses her shit laughing at me.

"Oh, Gina."

"This is gonna hurt, Spence. It's gonna hurt so fucking bad. It already does."

"Or," she drawls out, "maybe you're finally right where you belong."

"Nuh-uhn," I say, blowing my nose into the napkin on my tray. "Don't you start filling my head with more bullshit than what is already there. I need you to make me laugh. Like right now, before Jeff wakes up and comes in here and sees this ugly, blubbering mess."

"You'll never guess what your godson did last night," Spence finally starts, and I can already tell it's gonna be good.

"Which one?"

"Savage." Oh, his stories are always the best.

"What?"

"So, he was bathing in my tub last night, while I was watching TV in my room, and all of a sudden he's screaming his little ass off..."

"What happened?"

It takes her a moment to stop laughing before she continues. "So, he shouts, 'Mom, Mom, you have to come see this,' and of course I'm already out of the bed rushing to see what all of the fuss is about." Spence snorts. "I walk in, and he's standing butt-ass naked in the tub, bent over, trying to see between his legs."

"Oh, God. I'm scared."

"H—his hand is all up under there, and he's poking his ball sack, so I'm all, 'What the hell are you doing, Kyle?' and he lifts his head, serious as shit, and says, 'Remember when I told you I lost my marbles? I musta swallowed two of 'em, cuz I found 'em. They're in my nuts!'"

Chapter Thirty

JEFFREY

"Daddy, we maked you breakfast," Willow squeals, meeting me at the door when I return from my morning run.

I pat her little head, not wanting to pick her up and get her covered in sweat. "That was really nice of you. Thanks, pumpkin."

"Hey, Daddy," Evangeline says, smiling over at me from where she's washing dishes. "Good run?"

"Yeah. Thanks for breakfast. I'm gonna go shower real quick before I eat."

When I open my bedroom door, I find Tink, with the phone pressed to her ear, in absolute hysterics. There are actual tears streaming down her face.

I love it. I love every single thing about this moment. I love having her here in my home. I love her waking up in my bed. The sound of her laughter. The sight of her bed-tangled hair in the morning.

She looks toward the door, and our eyes meet. "Hey, Spence,

I'll talk to you later. Jeff just walked in...Thank you. Love you too. I will. I will. Okay, bye."

"You didn't have to hang up for me," I say, stalking toward the bed. "I didn't mean to interrupt." Careful not to rub my sweat all over her, I lean over and kiss the top of her head. "I'm just going hop in the shower real quick."

"It's fine," she says, dabbing the tears from her eyes. "I'm sorry I passed out on you last night. I don't even remember coming to bed."

"That's because you didn't," he chuckles. "You and the girls passed out in that chair. I was tempted to leave you, but you'd have all woken up sore this morning, so I snapped a couple of pictures then carried you to bed."

"Well, thank you. I didn't realize how tired I was."

"It's fine..." It was more than fine actually. I can still see the three of them cuddled up in that chair when I close my eyes. "The girls brought you breakfast in bed?"

"They did," she says with a smile as she looks to the half-eaten tray beside her. "They're amazing."

"You're amazing."

Tink blushes, smoothing down her unruly curls as she looks up at me through heavy lidded eyes. "You're not too bad yourself."

I run a frustrated hand through my hair. "The things I wish I could do to you right now."

"How 'bout I join you?" she asks, looking to the locked door, then back to me, hopeful.

The thought of having sex while my girls are at home gives me anxiety, but it's not like they can walk in. My dick swells, helping to sway my decision. "I'd like that, Tink. Very much."

Beaming, she stands in the center of my bed, taking me

completely by surprise when she jumps right into my arms, and smashes her lips to mine. Ignoring the mess of eggs and milk that have just splattered across the room, I kiss her back, sliding my hands under her ass, and head for the master bathroom.

"Jeffrey," she moans as I set her on the edge of the counter, still standing between her legs. My hands grip her hair, and our tongues duel for control. It's been over a week, and we're both crazy with want. I suck her tongue into my mouth, and she nips my lower lip. "You're salty," she giggles, licking her own lips before pressing them back to mine.

"I'm disgusting," I counter, unable to believe she's not put off by my current state.

"No," she groans. "You're delicious." Her tongue sneaks back in, licking the roof of my mouth. "You're perfect."

"Far from it," I argue, pulling my mouth away long enough to yank my shirt over my head. "I'm the worst possible man for you, Tink," I say, panic rising in my chest, because I hear what I'm saying, and I know it's the right thing to say. But I can't bear the thought of her actually leaving me. "You shouldn't settle for this."

Her teeth clamp down on her lower lip seductively as she reaches for the drawstring on my pants. "I want you so bad, Jeff. No matter how many warning signs my brain fires off. You're all I want anymore."

My hands grip her hips, which are now writhing against my waist. Ghosting my fingers up her sides, I bring her top along with them and pull it over her head. "I don't want to hurt you."

Her lip quivers, letting me know it's a fear we both share. "How 'bout you let me be the one to worry about that, huh?" Gina hooks her toes into the waistband of my underwear, sliding them down my legs. "Now, less talking," she growls, while running her hands up my sides. "More fucking."

Just as her teeth clamp down on the lobe of my ear, sending a chill shooting down my spine, I slide her off the counter, carrying her into the large walk-in shower. With her legs wrapped around my hips and her back pressed into the tile wall, I reach over to turn the water on, not anticipating the ear-piercing scream that comes from her mouth.

"Shhh," I dip my head, covering her lips with mine—kissing her into silence. Tink's hands grapple at my shoulders and chest, her nails digging into my skin while her tongue stabs at mine in lust and anger.

Once the water has warmed and the shower is steaming, she pulls back narrowing her eyes. "That was fucking cold," she hisses. "Don't do that shit."

"I'm sorry, babe...wasn't thinking. I'm used to it." There is nothing more refreshing after a couple-mile run than feeling that first burst of cool water hit my back. Apparently Tink doesn't share that opinion.

Little rivulets of water trickle down her face, and her breathing becomes labored, coming out in heavy pants as she licks the condensation from above her lips. She's so fucking beautiful like this that it makes it hard to breathe. She's in my arms, wrapped around my body, and still I can't seem to get close enough.

Tink shakes her head as she reaches over to the soap dispenser, filling her hand with body wash. Her eyes stare deep into mine as she works it into a lather and begins smoothing it over my shoulders and chest. Then she reaches lower, for my dick, and fists it into her palm, jerking it, her eyes flaming with desire.

My fingers dig into her ass as I rock against her. The heat

that's building in my stomach begins moving lower, filling my cock. "That's so good, Tink. So. Fucking. Good," I growl.

She lifts herself higher, sinking back down on my dick, taking it to the hilt. "Oh, Jeffrey," she gasps. Bracing her hands on my shoulders, she bounces up and down, her perfect tits brushing against my lips with every stroke.

Gina arches her back, riding me harder. She reaches between us to rub her clit while I suck the nipple of one of her breasts into my mouth, rolling my tongue around the hard bud. When her body starts to quake and I know she's almost there, I bite down gently, sucking hard as she explodes on my cock.

I'm dying to touch her, but my hands are occupied with holding her up. I'm completely at her mercy. "Tink," I rasp when I've reached the point of no return. "I'm gonna..." With a groan, I bite down on her shoulder, jerking my hips, and everything goes black as my release shoots out, filling her pussy.

"THAT WAS A LONG SHOWER," Evangeline notes, eyeing me funnily as I take a seat at the table, preparing to eat my now ice-cold breakfast.

"Mmm," I garble over a mouthful. "Got caught up talking with Gina. What do you girls think of a movie night?"

Willow looks over her shoulder from the play kitchen across the room, beaming. "Oh, yes, Daddy. I wuv moobies!"

"Good morning," Gina singsongs as she strolls into the kitchen, giving a little twirl in the center of the room. She's so girl-like. I can't think of a better word to describe what I mean. She's *all* woman in the areas where it really counts, but there's this happy-go-lucky aura that surrounds her. It just makes you feel good to be in her presence. Gina's hair is blown dry and in loose waves down her back. She's wearing a short floral sundress and not a drop of makeup. The sun seems to highlight the faint dusting of freckles on her cheeks. How haven't I noticed those before? I want to kiss each one.

Dear God, I can't stop staring.

Scrubbing a hand over my face, I try to regain my wits. "Look who decided to get out of bed," I tease, attempting to throw Vangie off our scent. I'm sure it's just my paranoia that's getting to me, but she seems a little suspicious, and I'm staring like some lovesick fool. *Get it together, Jeff.*

Tink heads straight for the Keurig to brew herself a cup of coffee, and my girls flock to her sides. A pang of guilt strikes my chest. I wonder what Jessica thinks of the relationship she's building with our girls. Of the relationship *I'm* building with this woman. My breath starts coming in shallow pants. It's only been three years. Is that enough time? Am I a horrible man for feeling...*feelings* for another woman? If I truly loved Jessica, the way I know I did—how? How can this be happening?

"Hey, girls," I say, my chair screeching across the floor as I spring up, unable to stay still. My forehead breaks out in a cold sweat. "I'm gonna go run to the store and pick up a movie candy buffet and something to cook for dinner tonight. I'll be back." Their responses barely register in my addled mind. I hope they didn't ask anything important, because I've just completely missed it.

Chapter Thirty-One

GINA

"Hmm," Vangie mutters watching her dad rush out of the door without a backward glance. "That was weird."

"Him didn't even ax me what I want. How rude," Willow complains, resting a hand on her hip and cocking it out to the side. *Little Miss Thang.*

Jeff's rapid departure has me feeling all sorts of insecure. He went from appearing happy and content to full-on panicked. Maybe what just happened in the shower was too much? I shouldn't have thrown myself at him while the girls were home. I knew he wasn't ready. *Shit.* "I'm sure he just had something important to take care of, girls. Maybe a work call or something on his way out. Who knows?" I'm trying to sound cool as a cucumber as to not worry the kids more than they already are, but I'm secretly burning up inside.

To pass the time, I decide to give the girls makeovers. We start with manis and pedis. Then full makeup and hair. By the time we finish, he's still not back. It's been hours, and the store is only a few miles away.

"It's not like Dad to be gone so long and not call. You think he's okay?" Evangeline asks, clearly upset by her father's odd behavior.

"I'm sure he's fine. Why don't you go put Willow down for a nap, and I'll clean up this mess?" I wave my hand, gesturing to the lipsticks and polishes littering the counter. Willow really had a field day with my Kaboodle.

Once the girls have disappeared up the stairs, I grab my phone, and with my heart lodged in my throat, call him.

"Hey, Tink." Jeffrey answers on the second ring. His voice is strained. I can tell he's trying to sound like nothing's wrong, but he fails miserably.

"Jeff?" I hate that my voice cracks when I say his name and I absolutely despise feeling vulnerable. "Is, umm. Is everything okay?"

After a slight pause, he sighs. "Yeah...I just needed a minute to clear my head. I'm sorry for leaving like that...I uh—I went to visit Jess at the cemetery."

"Because of me?" My heartbeat is drumroll in my chest as I await his response.

"I'm not sure how to answer that."

The back of my throat begins to burn. "The truth, Jeffrey."

"The truth is that I miss her." I know this already, but hell if it doesn't hit me like a hammer to the chest. "And I'm struggling with the feelings I have—for you," he adds, sounding completely defeated.

"Do you want me to go?" I don't want to, but I don't want to be an added source of pain in his life either. This isn't supposed to hurt like this. My heart shouldn't feel so tight in my chest. I shouldn't feel so afraid.

"No." His answer is brief, but immediate, and said with enough conviction that I believe he really wants me here. I knew this wouldn't be easy. It's not realistic for me to expect his feelings for his wife to just disappear because I'm in the picture. So, I stay.

"Okay," I whisper, squeezing the phone tightly in my palm. "See you soon."

"Was that my Dad?" Vangie asks, sneaking up behind me, nearly scaring me half to death.

"Yeah." My hand draws to my chest in surprise and I take a few deep, soothing breathes, and force myself to smile. "He said he'd be back soon...What do you say we get started on this movie marathon without him?" I ask, wrapping my arm around her shoulders and pulling her toward the living room.

Vangie and I watch the new *Jumanji* movie with Jack Black, Kevin Hart, and The Rock, since it's not at all appropriate to watch with Willow. I try really hard to focus on not thinking about Jeffrey, which is totally counterproductive. This sick feeling in my chest just won't go away.

Midway through the movie, Evangeline gets a bad case of cramps, so I fix her up with the heating pad and some meds and curl up beside her on the couch.

"Did you talk to my dad yet about taking me to the doctor for birth control?" Vangie asks.

"No. I didn't get a chance, but I'll talk to him soon, okay?"

"Birth control?" Jeff's voice roars from behind the couch.

Evangeline and I both jump up, staring at each other with stunned faces. I didn't even hear him come in. "It's not what you—" Oh, God. That sounded so bad. So, so, so bad.

"She's fucking fourteen, Gina!" Jeff's eyes are hard and accusing. "Who gave you permission to talk to my little girl about getting on birth control? That shouldn't even be a thought in her head at this age."

"I wasn't—" I try to defend myself, but Jeffrey is pissed beyond reason.

"Don't!" he shouts, cutting me off again. "I know what I heard. Don't even try to convince me otherwise." He runs a shaking hand through his hair, glaring at me. And it hurts. Dear God does it pierce my soul to be sneered at with such derision by the man who's come to occupy my every waking thought.

"Just listen to her, Daddy," Evangeline begs with huge tears pouring down her face. She looks like a little doe caught in headlights. No clue where to turn or what to do.

"Go to your room, Evangeline."

She hesitates, looking to me with helpless bewilderment.

"Now!" he shouts, stomping his foot. I have never seen him so angry, and as much as it hurts that he's yelling at me, it pisses me off to no end to see the way he's breaking his daughter's heart.

"Just, go, baby. I'm fine." I kiss the side of her face, breathing in her sweet scent. I try to commit it to memory, knowing this will be the last time I ever see her. My heart splinters in two as I watch her run off sobbing. I will not be the source of this kind of pain in his children's lives. They don't deserve this.

"I knew I couldn't trust you." His words are knives, cutting me deeper than I think he even realizes. He was already having a rough day and I know that he's looking for any reason to explode, but I can't do this. I *won't* do this.

"Did you?" Crossing my hands on my chest, I stare into his eyes with a heavy swallow.

"You're not her mother. You had no right..." His head drops, shaking side to side. Then he points roughly up the stairs. "They had a mother. They had an amazing mother."

"I'm aware," I say, clearing my throat, fisting my hands at my sides to absorb some of the tension running through my body.

"Of all people to bring around my girls, I choose you?" He begins pacing the room. "A woman with no morals. A fucking sex therapist!" He spits my title out like it's something dirty—something to be ashamed of, and I stand there with tears building in my eyes, too shocked to do more than take it. "I should have known with the way you reacted when I told you about them kissing on the cruise." His head shakes at the memory, and he exhales a humorless laugh. "With the way you threw yourself all over me. My God, Jessica is probably turning in her grave."

That does it. "If she's turning in her grave for any reason, it's for the way you just treated her daughter," I say, finally catching my wits.

"Don't you dare talk to me about how I raise my daughter. You have no fucking clue how to raise a child. And if that wasn't obvious before, it is blatantly so now."

I scoff. "You called and practically *begged* me to help you with her, and I came. Then, you called me again, and here I am. You obviously didn't think me too bad of a role model then."

"My mistake."

I nod, staring right into his eyes as tears fall from mine. "Make damn sure you never make that mistake again."

He snorts. "No worries. From now on, we stick to the original arrangement."

Is he fucking insane?

"No," I counter with a shake of my head. "From this moment

forward, there is no *arrangement*."

He has the audacity to look hurt. "What are you saying, Tink?"

"You told me to let you know if it became too much," I say, slipping my feet into my shoes without losing eye contact. "This, Jeffrey, and you...it just became too fucking much."

He follows me to the bedroom, watching me throw all of my things back into my bag, and he's seething. It's like there's a raging bull in the room, sucking up all of the air. It's stifling.

"I can't believe this shit." He runs his hand over the top of his dresser, knocking all of its contents to the floor. "You're really going to punish me for being upset over what I just walked in on?"

"Jeffrey." My voice is eerily calm. I just don't have it in me to fight with this man. My heart is already breaking, and I haven't even left yet. It's taking all I have to keep from falling to pieces in front of him. "You're not a child, any more than I am." I give him a pointed look. "And I would never do anything to punish or hurt you. But this," I say, eyeing his still-shaking form, "this is more than I can handle."

"Don't do this..." He grips my wrist, his face softening. And I want nothing more than to melt into his arms. For him to take it all back and kiss it better. But, I'm not naive enough to believe this won't happen again.

"I didn't," I say, yanking my arm out of his hold and throwing my purse over my shoulder. "Goodbye, Jeffrey."

Chapter Thirty-Two

JEFFREY

She's gone.

This splintering pain in my chest is forcing me to face what I've been fighting to admit to myself—I've fallen in *love* with her. The guilt I was drowning in suddenly takes a back seat to the realization that I've lost her and likely, for good.

Oh, I'm still mad as fucking hell. Furious even. With her. With myself. With life.

"Gigi, I waked up!" The sound of Willow's bare feet slapping the wood steps echoes throughout the house.

Shit. Suddenly, I'm feeling so ashamed.

"Hey Daddy-oh," my little girl chirps, a grin from ear to ear. "Where Gigi? It's moobie time!" She breaks out into a little jig, half Cabbage Patch, half Carlton.

My heart screws up tight and I feel hot all over. Tugging the collar of my shirt away from my neck, I try to find air. "She uh...she had to go, baby."

"Huh?" Willow's smile vanishes, and her pretty blue eyes well with tears. "Her leaved already? Before moobie night?"

When the tears start to flow, I pick her up, holding my little girl tightly to my chest. I don't know whether I'm trying to comfort her or myself as I smooth my hand in soothing circles over her back.

"But, I was gonna sweep wif her tonight, Daddy." Her face lifts from my shoulder, and she stares right into my eyes. "Her promised."

"It's not her fault, Willow. Dad made her leave." Vangie's arms cross on her chest, and the eyes I'm met with hold nothing but disgust.

"Don't do this, Evangeline," I beg. "You don't have to hurt her because you're angry with me."

"You told Gigi to go home? Why?"

I feel like I'm stuck at the bottom of a ravine with no way out. There's nothing I can say to make her understand. She's three.

"Because he's jealous, Willow. He doesn't want anyone else to love us."

Tears burn the backs of my eyes, and bile rises in my throat. *Is this what my daughter truly believes?* My head shakes side to side—in disagreement or denial? I'm not even sure I know the answer to that. "That's not true," I argue, wanting to believe I'm not that egotistical.

"No?" My daughter huffs out a long breath. "She was the best thing that ever happened to this family since...since..." she stammers, tears lining her cheeks. "Since Mom died. And you just threw her away."

"You tan tall her back and say sowwy, Daddy." Ah, the innocence of a toddler.

"It's more complicated than that, princess. Grown-up stuff."

Vangie snorts, and I get that she's upset, but so am I, and

this is not the time to have this discussion.

"Evangeline Elise, I understand you're angry, and we can talk more later, but you will not discuss another word of this in front of your sister. Do you understand me?" It pains me to yell at her. She's already looking at me like she despises the ground I walk on.

"Whatever, I'm out." *Who is this child?* I think to myself as I watch her storm off, back to her room.

"I really yike Gigi, Daddy," Willow whispers. "Her painted my nails and my toes, and her tisses and snuggles me yike a real momma."

And the hits just keep on fucking coming. "I'm glad you like Gigi, honey. But, you know she's not your momma. Your momma's in heaven with Jesus." I smooth the hair back from her face, wiping her tears away with my thumbs. "And I know that Mommy wishes more than anything to be able to kiss and snuggle you."

Willow groans, exasperated by my response. "I know dat hers not my momma. I said her wuvs me yike a momma. Yike a *tend* one."

"I'm sorry, princess." I don't know what else to say. I should have never brought her around my kids. It's one thing to hurt myself, but to know I've added more grief to their lives unnecessarily...I hate myself for it.

"I wuv you, Daddy." Her little arms latch around my neck, offering me comfort when I need it most.

"I love you too, Willow Jane."

Evangeline remains in her room for the remainder of the evening—not even coming down when I call her for dinner. Willow and I hang out in my bed, watching movies and eating our feelings, as Gina would say. The great thing about three

206 ♦ HEATHER M. ORGERON

year olds is their short attention span. Once I distract her with junk food and cartoons, she's all about it. Her sister, however, will be a lot harder to win over.

When she finally passes out, a little after nine, I head up to Evangeline's room. I feel like I'm walking into a snake pit.

Tap. Tap. Tap. I knock, softly, not all that confident she will even respond.

"You were dating her, weren't you?" Vangie asks, pulling the door open. My little girl is more observant than I give her credit for.

"Yes."

She nods, moving aside so I can walk past.

Vangie plops down on the edge of her bed, so I turn the desk chair to face her and settle in for what I'm sure will be a grueling conversation.

"Just so you know," Vangie starts, pulling her pillow into her lap and hugging it tightly to her chest. "She wasn't trying to get me on birth control because I want to have sex."

My eyes widen.

"I *don't* want to have sex, Dad."

"Oh, thank God."

With a roll of her eyes, she continues. "She said she was gonna talk to you about taking me to a gynecologist because my cramping is really bad, and sometimes they can put you on the pill and it helps."

Gina wasn't trying to undermine me. She wasn't encouraging my daughter to explore her sexuality. In a moment of clarity, I can't even fathom how I ever thought that's what she intended in the first place. Gina was only concerned about my daughter's well-being. Doing exactly what I called on her to do. If I'd listened. If I'd allowed her two fucking minutes to explain...

Goddamn it!

"What have I done?"

My daughter gives me an "I told you so," look and I can't even be mad at her. I deserve so much worse. "You have to get her back, Daddy."

"I'm not sure I can, Vangie."

"Do you love her?"

I shrug, unable to say the words to my child. That I've fallen in love with a woman who is not her mother. I can barely admit it to myself, but the look on her face tells me that my confirmation isn't needed.

She dangles her feet over the bed, edging closer to where I sit. "Loving Gina doesn't mean you can't love Mom, too. And it doesn't mean you have to love one more or less. Do you love me more than Willow because I came first?"

"No."

"Do you feel guilty for loving her just as much?" she asks, her eyes meeting with mine. "No, Dad, you don't. Because your heart is big enough to love a lot of people at the same time. I'm not afraid of Gina taking Mom's place. That will belong to her forever, but we can give Gina her own place," my wise-beyond-her-years daughter says with tears streaming down her face. "I won't stop myself from being close to other people because I'm afraid I'll hurt Mom, and you shouldn't either. Mom can see what's in our hearts, and she knows she's still in there."

Schooled on love by a fourteen-year-old. "When did you get so smart?" I ask, swiping at the first tears I've shed in front of my child since the day we buried her mother.

"Good genes."

Chapter Thirty-Three

GINA

"Heya, Gina," Josie yells out above the crowd when I burst through the door at T-Boys. Ignoring the rest of the customers lining her bar, she waltzes right over to me with a shot of Fireball in hand. "Where's lover boy and his kidney scraper tonight?" My ridiculous friend holds her hands out, thrusting her hips forward a few times.

"Hey, babe." I lift the shot to my mouth, ignoring her question. The familiar burn of whiskey swimming down my throat says peace is just around the bend. I've shed my last tear for that motherfucker. If I can avoid thinking of him, talking about him, or being anywhere within a five-hundred-foot radius of him, I should have no trouble keeping this promise to myself. Me and whiskey...we got this.

"They're pretty good." I dip my head toward the stage, referring to the '80s cover band who are belting out a shockingly good rendition of *Don't Stop Believin'* by Journey. They must be new.

Josie drops my usual Crown and Coke and another shot of

Fireball in front of me. "Yeah, lead singer's pretty easy on the eyes, too," she gushes, resting her chin in her hands and staring after him. I swear the girl has little pulsating cartoon hearts in her eyes.

"Don't do it, Josie-girl. Men are nothin' but trouble." I take the second shot into my still-shaky hand and swallow it down. Fuck you, Mr. Ryan. You might have stolen my heart and destroyed it beyond repair...But I'm not giving you my shot, too.

"Trouble in paradise?" Nosy Josie pries while reaching beneath her bar to get the dude beside me a beer.

"You know...even the biggest, thickest, veiniest cock isn't worth putting up with the dick attached to it after a while." I catch myself gesturing with my hands to the size of that glorious penis, and quickly shove them under my ass, sitting on them, when the mouth of the guy beside me drops almost to the floor.

"I dunno, girlfriend. I might be willing to put up with a whole lotta bullshit for a dick that big and *girthy*." Josie's blue eyes widen, and she gives an exaggerated shiver. "Mmm. I'm getting pregnant just thinking about it."

"You're a freak."

"Look who's talkin'," she teases before rushing over to the other end of the bar, where her customers have become impatient. I'm not used to this place being so busy, and I'm more than a little bummed that Josie can't keep me company. The last thing I want is to be left alone with my thoughts.

"Well, well, Gina Bourque. Isn't this a pleasant surprise?" *Oh God. I know that voice.*

With a fake-ass smile, I spin in my stool. "Brent. How ya been?"

He shrugs, gesturing to the empty stool beside me, "Mind if I sit down?" *Yes.*

"Not at all." My eyes give him a good once-over, and I can't for the life of me figure out what I ever saw in this young boy. Sure, he's all muscly and tan. Teeth are nice...bright and straight. "How's school going?" I ask, and it feels like I'm talking to a child, instead of a man. A man I've fucked. Ew. Okay, now I'm just freaking myself out.

"Good. It's going good." Brent smiles, staring at me all googly-eyed. "What've you been up to?"

Like magic, another shot appears before me. *Gotta love Josie.* Before answering, I shoot it, chasing it down with the rest of my drink. "Bring me another, Josie!" I shout, banging the empty glass on the bar a few times.

When I turn back to the side, that boy is still there, staring at me as if waiting for something. "I'm sorry? Did you say something?"

Brent chuckles. "I asked where you been? Haven't been seeing you 'round."

"Me?" I laugh. Then, my eyes sweat a little as I remember where I have been the past few months. In Jeff's bed. In my bed...with Jeff. The cruise. Nola. I cough, clearing my throat and my head. "Well, I've been getting my heart broken, Brent. Can't say I recommend it."

"I'm a good listener if you wanna talk about it." He props his elbow on the bar top, resting his head in his hand, while tilting his face to the side. He hits me with those whiskey brown puppy dog eyes. Did that really turn me on before?

"Nope," I say, swiping the drink my girl just put in front of me from the bar. "I wanna dance."

Wiggling through the crowd, I make my way right up front

and center. Sweat-soaked bodies bang up against mine as they dance without a fucking care in the world. I can't wait for my buzz to hit—to drown this dreadful heartbreak in alcohol. To be blessedly numb to this godawful pain. To feel as good as these drunk sons of bitches who got a head start on me.

"Hell, yeah," I shout when the beginning chords to "Pour Some Sugar on Me" by Def Leppard flow through the speakers. The familiar beat moves through my body. With my eyes closed, I throw my hands into the air and imagine Jeffrey's chest pressed to my back, his fingers creeping up my sides and cupping my tits. His mouth on my neck—sucking, tasting, teasing.

"Open up," he rasps into my ear, nibbling the lobe. The bottom of a shot tube runs along my lips, and I open, welcoming the burn. I'm not sure what he just gave me, but it goes down smooth and further heats my blood. I'm so hot. So tingly and horny. *I am so fucking horny.*

Song after song, we remain out on that dance floor, fucking with our clothes on, and I can't wait to bring him home...or well, he should probably take me home, because I am fucking trashed. And he'd better apologize, because I can't remember why, but I'm mad at him. Really fucking mad. But, he's such a good dancer. And I love him. I. Love. Him.

"God, you're hot," he says, spinning me around and draping my arms over his shoulders. Blinded by tears, we sway side to side to "Open Arms." Then he's kissing me and touching me in all the right places.

"Mmm," I moan, trying to eat his face. Oh God, I want him so fucking bad.

"Gina!" Spencer shouts, ripping me from the arms of my dark prince. *What the hell is she doing here?*

"Hey besssstieee," I slur, giggling because my voice sounds

so funny. Like I'm under water. "He came. He came for me."

"Who came for you, babe? What are you doing?" Spencer can be so dense sometimes. Those kids are eating up all her brain cells.

With my eyes, I motion over my shoulder. "Jeffrey, derrr."

"Whoa," I say, holding out my hands for balance when she yanks me over to the wall.

"That isn't Jeffrey, Gina. I've never seen that guy before, and can I just say, *ew*. I can't believe you let that nasty guy kiss you."

"What? What are you talking about?" Spence has gone off her rocker because that was Jeff. Wasn't it?

My bestie lets out an aggravated growl, and I kinda wanna tit-punch her because just who the fuck does she think she is, cock-blocking me? "Let's go." She pulls on my arm, dragging me toward the exit.

"Wait. Wait, Spence." I dig my heels into the floor, trying to pull her back. "Get Jeffrey, please."

"Gina," she groans, pinching my cheeks together like she does to the twins when she wants them to look at her. I'm not her fucking kid. I'm a responsible adult, dammit. "Listen to me."

"I'm lishunin," I mutter through fish lips. She's squeezing my mouth so damn hard...I bet it'd hurt if I were capable of feeling anything.

"That dude was not Jeffrey. I don't know where Jeffrey is, and I'm sorry for whatever he did to you. But that was not Jeffrey." A tear drips down my best friend's cheek. "Do you understand?"

Tears well up in my eyes, spilling over, and my best friend pulls me to her chest. She rubs my back. Kisses my cheek. "Where is he?" I cry, digging my nails into her back.

"Oh, honey. I don't know."

"But h—how did you know I was here?"

"Josie called. Some guy named Brent told her you were nursing a broken heart and was afraid that dude would take advantage of you." Her eyes dart back over to the dance floor.

A loud sob escapes my trembling lips. "Th—that really wasn't m—my CEO?"

"No," Spencer confirms, wrapping an arm around my shoulders and starting for the door. "That was something you'd have never touched sober. Ever."

Oomf! WHAT THE—? ALCOHOL SLOSHES in my belly.

"Auntie Gigi!" My throat burns as Kyle bounces around on top of me. *Where am I?*

I try to pry my eyes open, but the light is like a laser beam. So, I feel around, coming to the conclusion that I must've slept on my best friend's couch last night. "Savage," I groan. "Auntie's happy to see you too, but if you don't get off of me I'm going to—"

"Eww!" He leaps off the couch two seconds too late, and now he's dripping in vomit. "Daddy, Auntie frowed up on me!"

It's like the flood gates have opened, because no matter how hard I try to stop, it just keeps spraying from my mouth. From my nose. Oh, God, it burns so bad. I swear it's cooking the inside of my esophagus.

The sound of Cooper gagging only makes it worse. I'm gonna owe them a new couch, rug, hell maybe even a new house by the time this ends. I think maybe, I'm dying.

"Cooper, go give him a bath," Spencer orders, approaching

slowly with a huge gumbo pot. "Here, I don't see how there could be much left in that tiny stomach of yours, but try to get it in this please?"

"I'm so sorry," I finally groan once I've expelled every possible drop of alcohol from my body.

"Stop," she says, as she finishes wiping down the couch. "Coop can get the carpet, you come with me."

My best friend leads me up to her bathroom, runs me a bubble bath with candles, and pulls up a chair. "Get in and start talkin'."

So, I tell her all about the shit show at Jeffrey's house yesterday. About how he's not even close to coming to terms with the death of his wife and probably never will be. And that maybe I could have handled it, if it were just him and me and Jessica.

"Spence, I love those girls, but I'm afraid to try to have a relationship with them because I'll constantly have to worry that Jeff will blame me for the fact that Jessica isn't there to do it herself."

"Man, that's tough."

"Yeah, tell me about it."

"What're you gonna do?"

Shrugging, I sink down lower in the tub. "I'm already doing it."

Spence doesn't look to be at all impressed by my coping mechanism. "No repeats of last night, Gina. I don't wanna wake up to find your ass dead in a ditch one day." Her tone is light, but with one look at her face there is no mistaking how worried she is.

I have basically no recollection of last night, from the moment I stormed out of Jeffrey's house 'til Spencer was dragging me out of T-Boys. The look on my bestie's face tells me it's a damn good thing I don't remember.

"I mean it," she says, when I don't answer. "That guy was fucking creepy. You're hurt. I get it, but that is not the right way to handle it."

"Thank you for saving me, bestie."

She snorts.

"And I promise I'll handle it better."

"No more bars?"

Cut off my right arm why don't'cha. "Okay. But, I'll probably be over here a lot."

"Fine."

"And you'll have to keep me stocked on mommy porn," I giggle. "That shit's addictive."

Chapter Thirty-Four

JEFFREY

I t's been three weeks since I've seen her.

Held her.

Oh, and let's not forget, yelled at her like a goddamn idiot.

She won't take my calls...ignores all of my messages. But today, Tink won't be able to avoid me. It's Gina's thirty-sixth birthday, and through Landon and Evangeline, Spencer delivered our secret invitation. That's right—Gina has no clue we'll be there. I realize this could go very badly, but I'm desperate, and fairly certain she wouldn't do anything too unhinged around the children. But then again, this is Gina we're talking about.

"You have reached your destination." I'm a little alarmed when the navigation turns off before there's even a house in sight, but I continue down the winding path, finding it opens up to an expansive yard with some of the biggest, most beautiful oaks I've ever seen.

After shifting the truck into park, I twist around in my

seat toward the kids. "All right, girls. This is it. Remember everything we talked about?"

Evangeline's eyes roll. It's practically automatic anytime I speak to her these days. "Stay in the common areas. No closed doors. No sneaking off. No kissing."

"Good girl." Reaching around my seat, I ruffle her hair, which only further annoys her. This kid thinks she's so grown up, but it's my duty as her father to remind her that she's not.

"Willow?"

After adjusting the little tiara that accompanies every outfit these days she looks up at me and rolls her eyes, just like her sister. "No tissin' Tyle."

"Very good." Spinning back around to the front, I switch off the truck and open my door. The smell of meat on the barbeque hangs in the air, making my already nervous stomach growl. "Let's go."

"I told you Tyle was a prince, Daddy. He lives in a tastle!" Willow tugs my arm. Apparently I'm not moving fast enough for her.

The house is enormous. It's creamy yellow in color with stained glass windows and a wraparound porch. The architecture reminds me a lot of the homes in the Garden District, and that gets me thinking of Tink and the day we spent in New Orleans together. I think maybe that was the day I started to fall, and I've been tumbling ever since.

"Landon says to come around back," Vangie offers, tapping away at that damn cell phone that I regret ever giving to her before hauling ass to meet up with that boy.

"You made it." Spencer greets us with a huge, dimpled smile. "Come with me, and I'll introduce y'all to everyone."

Here we go. My hand tightens on Willow's as we follow

Gina's best friend over to the covered patio where she begins by introducing us to her mother and Cooper's parents.

Lois, the secretary at Gina and Spencer's office, who I've met a few times, walks over to say hello.

Then come Gina's parents, who I saw but was never actually introduced to at Dillon's house. "This is Gina's momma, Lydia, and her daddy, Chuck." There's something about these two that just gives me the heebie-jeebies.

"Nice to *officially* meet you both." As I'm shaking her father's hand, my eyes drift over his shoulder, toward the lake.

"She's fishing with Kyle...Why don't you and Willow walk over there and say hello?" Spencer's hand pats my shoulder a few times. "I'm gonna go have my son introduce me to that pretty daughter of yours, who I've heard so much about."

I hesitate for a moment, and Spencer giggles. "Go on...she won't bite. Well, not in front of the kids, anyway." Then she winks and gives me an encouraging little shove. "Willow will protect you."

As if in a trance, I amble across the yard with my heart taking up residence in my throat. It isn't until we've almost reached the dock that Tink finally sees us. She stands from where she's been fishing at the edge of the wharf, dusting off her bottom. Her long blonde hair whips in the breeze as she stares at us in disbelief. She's beautiful.

Our eyes lock, and a million different emotions rush through me all at once.

"What are you doing here?" Her brows furrow.

I keep walking 'til I'm standing about a foot away. *So close.* "Happy Birthday, Tink." Every nerve ending in my body is firing, aching to touch her. To hold her. To breathe her in. Damn, this is harder than I ever imagined. How do you go back to being strangers with someone you know so intimately?

"Happy Birfday, Gigi!" my baby girl squeals, dropping my hand and rushing over to hug her leg.

My heart tightens as Gina falls to her knees, enveloping Willow in her arms. "Thank you, sweetie. I've missed you so much. You just made this the best birthday, ever."

"'Sup, CEO?" Savage asks, laying his pole on the ground and walking over to give me a dab. "You got a lotta balls showing up over here today," the little shit says, loud enough that his godmother overhears and bursts out laughing so hard she nearly falls on her ass.

"We gotted you a present," Willow announces, glaring at Kyle for trying to steal her show.

Tink dabs at the corners of her eyes. "You did?"

"Mmmhmm." Willow nods, shoving the giftbag into her chest. "Here!"

I can tell by the way she's hesitating that she's uncomfortable accepting a gift from me. It's why I had Willow deliver it in the first place. She'd never refuse anything from her. The glare she shoots me lets me know she is completely aware of my little game.

Her hand dips into the bag, pulling out the black velvet gift box, and my pulse starts racing. I put so much thought into this present. I really hope she loves it. I *need* her to love it.

"It's a bracelet!" Willow shouts, spoiling the surprise. "Hurry, open it. I wanna show you my part."

"Oh, wow." Gina pulls the white gold bracelet out, fingering each dangling charm individually. A little cruise ship. A fleur-de-lis, representing our adventure in New Orleans.

"Daddy gotted you those," Willow offers. "Vangie picked the ice cream cone, cuz you taked her to eat ice cream when she gotted her wady business."

Gina's hand cups her mouth. I can't tell if she's laughing or crying. Either way, she's affected, and that's good.

"This one's mine! I gotted you the powish, cuz you painted my nails yike a mommy, and I don't have a mommy. So, that was special, right? Daddy said to pick somefin special."

"Oh, Willow..." Gina's hand flies to her mouth, and she gasps. "It's so special. Thank you." My baby giggles as Tink spreads kisses all over her little face. "You are so special to me, sweet girl. Please, don't ever forget that."

"You see, Kyle," I say, nudging him and pointing to the girls. "When a man screws up, he should have the balls to own up to it."

His little arms cross on his chest, tapping his foot as he looks me up and down. "Mr. Jeff, all due respeck—I think it's gonna take more than that bracelet to make her like you again."

"Then I'll do more, Kyle. I'm willing to do whatever it takes." Knowing that she's listening, I choose my words carefully.

"Well, you can prolly start with saying sorry to me, cuz you made Aunt Gigi frow up all over me."

Tink's mouth falls open, giving up all pretenses that she's not listening in. The flush in her cheeks starts spreading to her neck. Something tells me there's a hell of a story here, and one in which I am definitely not the hero.

"Willow, Kyle, I think I just heard them call you for ice cream!" She rounds them up, herding them down the pier and sends them running back toward the house.

"Can we talk?" I ask once the children have made it out of hearing distance. Her back is to me. Her arms crossed in a defensive stance.

Slowly she spins around. Her cheeks are tinged pink. Her

eyes glistening in the sunlight. "Jeffrey, don't do this."

"I have to." My voice sounds raspy to my own ears.

Tink's hands dig into her hair, and she tugs in frustration. "What do you want from me?"

"Everything." With a few strides, I'm standing inches away. My hands lift to frame her cheeks, and I feel her body begin to go limp.

Her head shakes slowly. "I can't," she rasps, clearing her throat. "I thought I could, Jeffrey, but I'm not strong enough to deal with all of this."

"I'm sorry, Tink." With my hand on the nape of her neck, I bring her head to rest on my chest, massaging gently. "I'm so fucking sorry for what I said. For the way I treated you."

Tilting her face up to mine with a finger, I lean in, pressing my lips to hers. Slowly, and reverently, I kiss her, until a soft, pained whimper pierces my heart. With her hands braced on my chest, she pulls back. Her tear-filled eyes make my chest constrict. "I can't do this. Stay away from me, CEO."

"How'd it go, man?" Cooper asks when I enter the kitchen to serve the girls lunch.

"Well," I say, running a hand through my hair. "She told me to stay away from her."

"No." Spencer interrupts, walking in from another room. "That is the very last thing you do. Gina doesn't know a good thing when it smacks her in the face."

"She comes off like a hardass," Coop offers, "but deep down that girl is as fragile as they come."

"Right." Spence smiles up at her husband in agreement,

wrapping her arm around his waist. "Like a flower."

"Yeah, or you know...a bomb." Coop snickers and jumps across the room in anticipation of the arm that nearly smacks him in the chest. *He's good.*

After giving her husband a pair of eyes, Spencer waves him off. "You hurt her, Jeffrey. Badly. Gina has never—ever—fallen for a guy the way she has for you, and it's not just you. She loves your kids too. Now you've got to find a way to prove to her this is more than sex."

"I told her—"

"*Show* her," Spence stresses. "Think *grand gestures*, Jeffrey."

Chapter Thirty-Five

GINA

"Hurry up, Gina," my best friend whines, peeking her head around into my office. "I'm starving."

I hold up a finger, indicating for her to give me a minute before I forget what I'm doing. "I'm coming." After I've finished writing in my last patient's chart and filing it away in the drawer, I grab my purse and follow her out to her car. "You know, he messaged me again today?"

"Who?" My best friend asks, looking over her shoulder as she pulls out of the lot.

"Who?" I mock. "Jeffrey, duh."

"What'd he say?"

I dig my phone from my purse, swiping my finger across the screen to open up the texts. "He said: 'Good morning Tink. I miss waking up with your tits pressed to my chest and my dick buried in your belly. Hope you have an amazing day at work.'"

Spencer snorts, nearly pulling her truck off the road. "Oh my God. He's awesome, Gina. Did you reply this time, or just ignore him again?" It's really starting to annoy me that she's so

Team Jeffrey. She's supposed to be on my side.

"What do you think?" I ask, shoving my phone back into my bag. "He's just missing my sexual prowess, is all."

"Uh. No offense, Gina, but he's really fucking hot. If all he wanted was pussy, he could pick that shit up at any bar or church in Livingston." Her eyes swoop to the side, looking at me pointedly. "And you know it."

I shrug, staring out the window. "I'm not talking to you anymore."

"Why? Cuz you know I'm right."

"Cuz you're a mean, skanky ho. That's why."

"Hey, Spencer...Gina," Lucy says, grabbing two menus and silverware, "Your friend beat you here."

Friend? "Friend...you didn't tell me someone else was meeting us for lunch."

Spence shrugs, following Lucy around to the back of the boat, my favorite spot. *Oh, God.* My heart starts jumping around in my chest erratically when I see *him.* He's facing away from us, but I'd know that back anywhere. Suddenly my appetite is gone. Or, rather, it's been replaced by another hunger entirely.

"Fuck this," I grumble, turning to haul ass out of this restaurant. I cannot handle this shit. *What the hell is he even doing here?*

"Oh, no, you don't." Spence's fingers close around my wrist, and she yanks. Hard. "You owe me lunch, and I chose Boudreaux's. We're eating here."

Jeffrey must hear the commotion, because he turns in his seat, his entire face lighting up when he sees us hissing at each other a few feet away. "Spencer," he says, coming over to join us. "Thank you so much for meeting me for lunch." He gives her a one-armed hug, kissing her cheek. And I'll be damned if my cheek doesn't burn with jealousy.

"Of course. I'm really excited to help you find the perfect place."

"Tink," he purrs. "I didn't realize you'd be here, but damn...I'm so happy you decided to join us." He looks like a little kid in a candy store. Well, he can just pick that panty-melting smile up right the hell now.

My head jerks back before I get the urge to do something stupid like throw myself into his arms and rip his clothes off. "Uh, I didn't decide shit." Narrowing my eyes at my *former* best friend, I add, "I have no idea what you're doing here or what this business you two have going on is even about. But, trust me, if I'd have known, I wouldn't be standing here right now."

Jeffrey leans in close, invading my personal space, effectively making my pulse race. His breath is warm against my cool skin, giving me a chill when he whispers into my ear, "You're so fucking sexy when you're flustered, Tink." His breath is all minty and fresh. I want to lick him and punch him and...and fuck him.

No. No, no, no. Calm down, kitty. So what if we haven't had sex in a bajillion years?

"I hate you," I growl at Spencer, as I take my sex-starved ass over to the chair farthest from his.

Peering over the menu that I'm only using as a shield, I watch Jeffrey bend to sit, adjusting his tie. His white, pin-striped oxford fits his muscled chest like a glove. And his pants...It should be considered indecent to fill the crotch of a pair of pants the way this man does. *Show off.*

"You okay, Gina?" Spencer asks, fighting back a laugh.

"Yeah, why?"

She snickers. "You fan that menu any harder and you're gonna fly right offa this boat."

Shit. Busted. Blinking a few times, I tear my gaze from his. I didn't even realize I was fucking staring. Way to make an ass of yourself, Gina.

"See anything you'd like to try?" Jeff adds, smirking, as I tear my eyes away from him. "I hear the sausage is *wonderful.*"

"Been there, done that. Got the scars to prove it." I do my best not to react when his face falls. I don't know why the hell I'm suddenly feeling guilty. Why can't I just hate him? This would be so much easier if he was some monster.

"Tink," Jeff rasps, reaching across the table for my hand. I want to pull it away. I *should* pull it away, but it feels so fucking good—his skin on mine—even if it is only the palm of his hand. "Give me a chance. Just one—to show you how sorry I am." His fingers lightly rub back and forth, turning me into a big ball of mush. "I won't fuck this up again, baby."

"Excuse me," I say, my chair screeching as I push back from the table. "I need the restroom."

Chapter Thirty-Six

JEFFREY

"What the fuck, Jeffrey? Follow her…"

"Oh, uh, right…Okay." I get up, feeling like a complete asshole. "So, I should go *inside* the bathroom?"

Spencer's eyes widen, and she nods her head. "Yes, Jeffrey. Go!"

My pulse quickens as I jog after her. I have no clue what I'll say or do when I get there, but if Spencer thinks I should follow her then by God I'm going to listen. I need all the help I can get.

"Tink," I whisper-shout, when I pull the heavy door open. "You in here?"

"This is the ladies' room, Jeffrey. Go away." Her voice is raspy, thick with attitude that I know she's using to hide her emotions. Jesus, this woman is a hard nut to crack.

"Is anyone else in here? Speak now, cuz I'm coming in."

I hear Tink gasp from inside the stall. "Like hell you are, get out of here, stalker."

With a deep breath, I pull the door the rest of the way open, shutting and locking the deadbolt behind me.

"Did you ju—Jeffrey? Are you really in here?"

"Right here babe. You doin' number one or two? Give me some idea how long I gotta wait, cuz I'm dying to get my hands on you."

Gina groans. "I really wish I could drop a fucking deuce right now and smoke your ass outta here."

God, I've missed her. "Well, that would give a whole new meaning to the phrase, smokin' dat ass." I snicker.

The stall door flies open, and Tink stalks past me to the sink, squirting some foamy soap into her hands and working it into a lather.

"You, uh...forgot to flush."

"Because I didn't *use* the restroom."

"So, you just came here to get away from me?" I ask, moving to stand in front of the door. There's no way I'm letting her escape that easily.

Without answering, she stares at herself in the mirror, adjusting her black lace top and smoothing the invisible wrinkles from her tan pencil skirt.

"Talk to me, Tink." My throat feels tight. "Tell me what I can do. How I can fix this?"

Finally, she turns to face me, her black heels clomping on the tile as she moves to stand before me—the scent of her familiar perfume driving me wild. Tink raises a hand to straighten my tie, smoothing it down the front of my chest and my heart begins to jackhammer against my ribcage. "I can't compete with a ghost, Jeffrey," she whispers. "I wouldn't even know where to begin, and to be frank...I don't want to. I know I'm no saint—far from it. But I don't need to be reminded of that every single fucking day of my life when you look at me and wish I was her."

"I won't."

"You *do*."

"I don't," I insist, pleading with my eyes for her to believe me.

Gina's eyes drop to my waist, and her hands grip my belt buckle. "My body is all I have to offer, Jeffrey. It's all I can afford to gamble with."

"No." My hand lifts to brush the side of her face. "I want all of you. Everything."

"Take it or leave it, CEO. Final offer."

Staring deep into her eyes, I start to say no. This isn't what I want at all, but I see the way she's looking at me, like I'm everything she's ever wanted and can never have. With so much pain and lust. And dare I even fool myself into believing...love? If physical love is my way in, I'll take it. I'll give her my body and bare my soul to her in the process. "Okay."

"Okay," she breathes out in a sigh of relief. "Fuck me, Jeffrey," she orders, her fingers moving to unfasten my belt. "And make it fast, before our food gets cold."

With my hands on either side of her face, I pull her to me roughly, thrusting my tongue into her mouth as I back her up to the far wall. There's nothing gentle about the way I'm kissing her. It's rough and animalistic. It's pure desperation. Tink wars for control, but I don't let up. She wants to be fucked...I'll be the one doing the fucking.

With both hands, I grip the bottom of her skirt, lifting it all the way up. My breath hitches as I take a moment to admire her body, completely bared from waist down, apart from a skimpy little thong. I run the knuckle of one finger along her pussy, feeling her entire body tense against mine. Her breaths start coming in shallow pants, the mewling sounds escaping from deep within her throat, fueling my desire. With one quick pull, I rip the scrap of fabric from her body. "This is mine," I growl, feeling possessive and crazed with how much I want her. Only her.

"It's yours," she agrees, turning to brace herself with two hands on the wall. "Enjoy, CEO, cuz that's all you get." She thrusts her ass out, chewing her bottom lip as she stares back at me over her shoulder.

"The fuck it is," I growl, spinning her back around. "You're gonna look at me, Tink. You're gonna see my face when I make you come."

Tears well in her eyes as I cup her ass in my hands, lifting her until she's seated on my hips, right above my cock. Instinctively, her legs wrap around my waist. I feather kisses down her neck, waiting for her to take what she wants, and then I'll blow her fucking mind.

"God, yes," she moans, lowering herself down on my painfully hard erection. It's a slow and damn near torturous descent. With her arms wrapped tightly around my neck, she turns to the side and begins to rock.

Gripping her thighs, I lift her, 'til only the tip of my dick remains inside. "I said you will look at me when I fuck you," I grit out, fighting the urge to move.

"Don't do this Jeffrey," she begs. Her lower lip begins to quiver, and I take it into my mouth. This time when I sink into her warmth, she doesn't turn away.

Fucking her hard and fast, I deliver what I know she craves. Her finger dips between our joined bodies, circling her clit. Slowly at first, getting faster as the pressure builds. When I feel her inner walls contracting around my dick, I take what I need, spilling my seed deep inside while making love to her mouth.

Slowly her shaky legs lower to the floor, her arms still around my neck, her tongue still mating with mine. No longer needing my hands to support her weight, I brush the backs of my knuckles along the side of her face and down her neck, tenderly. I fill my starving lungs with as much of her as I can, and she doesn't pull away. No, she melts into me, her hands frantically touching every inch of my chest.

Bang. Bang. Bang.

"Fuck!" Gina hisses, righting her skirt as I shove my dick back into my pants, straightening my mussed suit as much as possible.

"Is someone in there?" *Bang. Bang.* "Lucy. The damn door's locked," a woman's voice shouts in annoyance. "I needa pee."

"Come on," I say, ushering Tink toward the door with my hand on the small of her back.

She gives me a look that says I'm crazy. "This is the women's restroom, Jeffrey. We can't just walk out together."

"We either walk out, or someone's unlocking that door and coming in. We're not coming out of this unscathed. Let's walk out with a little dignity?"

Still fooling with her skirt, she mutters, "We just fucked in a restaurant bathroom. We have no dignity left."

"But it was some *good* fuckin'." I tease, twisting the lock.

"What in tarnation?" the little white-haired woman shouts when Tink and I stroll out of the restroom together.

"Sorry, ma'am. Had some business to tend to." I let my eyes rove over Tink's body, slowly. "It's all yours now."

Gina's face flames bright red, and her elbow digs into my side. "What he means, Mrs. Guidry, is I had something in my eye, and he was helping me flush it out."

"You two are a little old for this shit, Gina Bourque. I would call your momma, but that hooker would probably throw a fuckin' party." She shakes her head. "It's no wonder you're so lost."

Gina snorts in agreement. "Sorry, ma'am." Then she gives my back a shove, hurrying us away from the old woman.

"Oh, I was flushing something out alright," I tease, unable to control my peals of laughter as we make our way back to join Spencer at our table.

"That was my seventh grade English teacher, asshole."

"Hey, guys," Spence singsongs. "Did you run into Mrs. Guidry? We had a good time catching up while y'all were—ummm—*occupied*." Her eyes take in our disheveled appearance and she smiles knowingly, giving me a thumbs-up.

Gina collapses into her chair, burying her head in her hands. "Yeah, she just caught us fucking in the bathroom."

"Ouch." Spence tries to cover her laughter for a moment, before finally just letting it go. "You know this is gonna be on the five o'clock news tonight, right?" she teases. "Probably all over Facebook already."

"Yeah, yeah." Gina waves her off, pushing the cold food in her plate around with a fork.

"Do you want me to order you something else?" I ask, when I realize she's not planning to eat it.

"I can take care of myself Jeffrey," she snaps.

"Soooo," Spence drawls, trying to relieve a little of the tension. "What time do you meet with the realtor?"

"Wait, realtor?" Gina's eyes grow wide with alarm. *Checkmate.*

Deciding it best to ignore her, I direct my attention to her friend. "In about an hour. I think I'm gonna put in an offer. The girls and I loved it."

"Landon told me y'all stopped to have a look on the way home from Gina's party," Spence continues, also pretending her best friend isn't about to have a coronary between us. "Well, let us know how it goes. I can't believe we're going to be neighbors."

"Neighbors?!" Tink shouts, her eyes bugging out of her head. "What the hell is going on?"

"Surprise! The girls and I are moving to Magnolia Lake."

Chapter Thirty-Seven

GINA

It's Friday night, and here I am in a threadbare tee with lounge pants and a top knot, settling in on the couch with a new book and a bag of Tootsie Rolls. I haven't been out in weeks. Not since the night I got trashed and puked all over Spencer's house, and my godson. It's not one of my prouder moments. The bar seems to have lost its appeal now that I'm not out on a dick hunt. I don't even miss it like I thought I would. It's like, what's even the point?

So, when I'm not meeting up with Jeffrey for a quick fuck—which has definitely been made easier by his close proximity, even if it does make for lots of awkward run-ins—I'm either binging shows on Netflix or with my nose stuck in a book. Spence's latest recommendation is *Bashful* by Lo Brynolf. It's about a girl who falls in love with her gay best friend, and I'm way too invested in finding out how this could possibly end in anything but disaster.

I'm just getting started on the second chapter when the message alert on my phone sounds.

CEO: You busy?

Me: Reading, why? What's up?

CEO: *winky face* *eggplant emoji*

My insides get all tingly and warm at the thought of what his message implies.

Me: Your place or mine? Where are the girls?

CEO: They're at Spencer and Cooper's for a movie night. Gotta pick them up at midnight. Can you come here?

Me: Sure...Give me an hour. I need to freshen up.

FORTY-FIVE MINUTES LATER, I'M TURNING down Jeffrey's long, winding driveway. My breath catches when I pull up to the house, which is nothing short of amazing, with its second-floor balconies and turrets. It reminds me of a castle. The house itself is very similar to Spencer's in style, but pale blue in color. The right corner of the wraparound porch, which I love so much, opens up into a beautiful gazebo. It's every girl's dream home.

Running my hand along the intricate railing, I make my way up the steps. Butterflies swarm around in my chest as I lift my hand to knock. Lines between us have been blurring. Jeff's made it no secret that he moved here to be near me. To show me how serious he is and that he wants to make this thing work. But I'm afraid and stubborn, to a fucking fault.

The sound of his footsteps approaching sets my pulse to racing. It's the same every time I see him—a rush unlike anything I've ever felt before. I guess I'd liken it to a little kid on Christmas morning, eager and bursting to open their gifts. But I already know what's inside, and the excitement never lessens.

"Tink." He says my name in greeting, with a Cheshire Cat grin. His head is the only part of his body I can see, the rest is hiding behind the door. "Come inside. It's chilly out."

Stepping into the foyer, I deposit my things on the console table. When I spin around, I nearly choke from sucking in so much air. This insane man is wearing a white apron and chef's hat, and *nothing* else.

"Wine?" Jeff offers, holding out a glass of my favorite red as if nothing is out of the ordinary.

Eyeing him from the top of his head to his bare toes, I take the offered drink. "What are you doing, Jeffrey? Is this...are we doing role-play?" I mean, I've never done anything like that before, but I would be down for any kind of sex with this man.

"Nope." He winks, motioning for me to follow him.

Lord have mercy, I want to reach out and squeeze those perfect, round ass cheeks. "Why aren't you wearing any clothes?"

His only response is a shrug.

"You're a strange man, Jeff—" My thoughts are lost when I step foot into the dining room. Vases of red roses sit on every surface—loose petals are scattered over the white linen table cloth. The only light comes from the candles at the center of the table, offering the perfect romantic atmosphere. I'm speechless. I've only seen the likes of this in the movies. Fucking frat boys doesn't lead to candles, roses, and wine.

"What do you think?" he asks, pulling out my chair.

My mouth opens and closes and then I get a glimpse of his bare ass as he moves to sit in the chair beside me and burst out laughing.

"Something funny?" He scoots his chair in and removes the silver dome lids covering our plates, revealing some sort of shrimp pasta in a white sauce. It looks and smells delicious.

"I don't know what's going on right now, Jeffrey." I glance around the room then back to his *outfit*. "You're eating this fancy dinner...wearing that?"

He looks down at his chest and back up to me. "Unless it bothers you."

"What's going on?" I'm so fucking confused. I can't tell if he's trying to woo me or making a fucking joke. If it's the latter...I just may kill him.

"I'm having a nice romantic dinner with the woman I love." Well, excuse me. Way to drop the L-word. Now I can't breathe.

"Wh—what's with the outfit?" He said he loved me. *He loves me?*

Jeff smirks. "I thought maybe I could distract you from your overactive mind. Is it working?"

With a hard swallow, I nod. "I th—think it might be, Jeffrey."

"Great!" He slaps his hands together a few times. "Let's eat."

"Eat?"

The confusing man laughs. "You know...put the fork in the plate, bring it up to your mouth. Chew. Chew. Swallow. Repeat."

"Jeffrey?" My whole world is spinning right now. I can't possibly eat.

"Yeah, babe?"

"Did you just—oh, God." Tears prick the backs of my eyes. My throat swells up. Don't you fucking do it, Gina. Don't you start crying like a damn fool. "Did you mean me?"

His brows furrow in confusion. "When?"

"Y—you said the woman you l—love."

Jeff looks around the room, under the table, behind his chair. "Is there another woman in this room I'm unaware of?" he teases. "Yes, Tink. Of course, I meant you."

"You love me?"

He reaches out, taking my hand into his. "Gina, I wouldn't have uprooted my children and bought a house in your best friend's neighborhood if I wasn't crazy in love with you."

"This is really happening..." I mutter beneath my breath.

"I lied to you, Tink." He reaches into the front pocket of his apron, retrieving a small red velvet pouch. He pulls it open, dumping something shiny into his hand. Then, he reaches for my wrist, lifting it into the air, and hooks another charm to the bracelet he and the girls gave me for my birthday. The bracelet I never take off. "When I said I couldn't give you my heart."

He removes his hand, and there's a white gold heart charm dangling beside the ship. Holy. Shit. "Jeffrey?" My own voice sounds foreign to my ears.

"You already have my heart, Tink. It's yours, and I want more than anything to possess yours."

"Jeffrey?" I say again. Apparently, it's my go-to response because I can't form a coherent thought, much less express it verbally.

"What'dya say, Tink? Can we give this a shot? Will you be my girlfriend?" he asks, all sheepish and boy-like.

"Oh, Jeffrey," I nod. Stupid tears spill down my cheeks. "I love y—you too."

"You do?" His beautiful blue eyes shimmer in the candlelight. "So, does this mean I can finally take you on real dates?"

"I'd like that."

"Wait 'til I tell the girls! They're going to be so excited."

Wait, what?

"Huh? You wanna tell your children? Are you sure, Jeffrey?" Alarm bells start going off in my head. This was where we fucked up last time.

"Of course I want to tell them, Gina. They love you too, and they've been very impatiently waiting for me to win you back." He chuckles. "In fact, it was Evangeline who made me finally realize that it's okay...to love you, I mean. I know that sounds fucked up, but I couldn't help feeling like I was somehow dishonoring my wife by falling in love with you. And I couldn't stop myself from falling...I was a fucking mess, and I will never forgive myself for hurting you, Tink."

"You want me, for real." I can't wrap my head around the level of permanence he's implying. He's talked to his kids about me. About dating me. About being in love with me. *He. Loves. Me.*

"I want you, Tink. God, I want you in every fucking way. I want you in my house and in my bed. At my breakfast table and sitting beside me at church on Sundays. I want your girly shit littering the counters in my bathroom and your soap in my shower." He gets up from his chair, and I try not to lose it over his bare ass again. Kneeling at my feet, he takes my hand into his, kissing each of my fingers one by one. "Say you're mine, baby. Just be mine."

"I'm yours, Jeffrey. God help you if you fuck this up." I laugh, rubbing my hand along his jaw. "I'm a little crazy, CEO. I hope you know what you're getting yourself into."

His response is to curl an arm under my knees and the other around my back, scooping me up from the chair. He carries me over to the living room, depositing me on a bed made of pillows and blankets right in front of the already-lit fireplace.

He literally thought of everything.

"Will you come with me to pick up the girls later? I want us to tell them together." Only Jeffrey would still be thinking of his children at a time like this.

"Yes," I rasp, pulling his face down so I can kiss his lips. "But...maybe you should put some clothes on first?"

Chapter Thirty-Eight

JEFFREY

"You two almost done up there?" I call up the stairwell as Spencer's truck rolls to a stop in front of the house. "That boy's here." Vangie hates it when I call him that.

Radio silence.

Tink and Vangie have been holed up in my bathroom for damn near three hours now getting ready for homecoming. It's her first school dance. Gina says it has to be perfect. She took her shopping for a dress and shoes last week. Took her to get her hair and nails done. And now she's doing her makeup. All of the things I'd never have even thought to do. All of the things she would have missed out on by not having her mother.

The doorbell chimes, and before I can even get to the foyer, I hear Willow. "Ooh Yannon. You wook yike prince sharmin!"

"Thanks, Willow."

"Y'all come on in," I say to Landon and Spencer. "She's still up there with Gina getting ready."

"I bet she looks amazing in that green dress with her red

hair," Spence says, all giddy.

"Why don't you go up there and try to hurry them along?" I suggest because I can tell she's just dying to be a part of this makeover, and I need a moment alone with her son.

"Lookin' sharp, bud," I say, admiring Landon's suit and tie.

"Thanks." He stares down at his feet. I'm making him nervous. That's good.

"Now that your mom is outta the way, we're gonna go over a few ground rules."

"Daddy, Gigi telled you to yeave Yannon alone." Willow wags her little finger at me, and Landon tries to cover a laugh.

"Listen here, Landon." His head comes up, and his eyes meet mine. "No kissing, no butt touching, no boob touching." I start ticking off all of my ridiculous rules on my fingers.

Landon's face turns beet red. "Yes, sir."

"Boy," I warn, getting in his face. "I know you've been kissing my daughter. You better cut that shit out."

"Yes, sir," he lies.

"Jeffrey," Tink growls on her way down the stairs. "I told you not to mess with him." Her eyes get all starry when she sees the boy she helped raise, all decked out. "You look like a little man. Oh my God. I think I might cry." Her hands wave in front of her face to dry the tears before they fall.

"Here she comes," Spence shouts down the steps, starting a drumroll as Vangie begins her walk down the stairs, making her grand entrance.

"Princess." My hand goes to my chest. She looks so beautiful—and so much like her mother—that for a moment it's hard to breathe.

"Wow," Landon rasps, his eyes about bugging out of his head at the sight of Evangeline all made up. "You look so beautiful, Vange."

Suddenly, Tink's arm hooks around my elbow. It's like she knows exactly what I need when I need it. Because seeing the way that boy is looking at my baby has me ready to call this whole ridiculous thing off.

"Thanks, Lan." Vangie blushes, leaning in to whisper something into his ear.

A smile curls his lips, and I want to know what the hell was just said. This growing up business is a load of bullshit.

"Calm down, papa bear," Tink teases. "They're going to a school dance, and Spencer is chaperoning. They aren't running off to the courthouse."

"Go stand by your dad in front of the fireplace, Evangeline. I wanna get a shot of you two together before we leave," Spencer orders, lifting the camera that's dangling around her neck and making adjustments to the settings.

"You look so beautiful, baby," I whisper, wrapping my arm around her shoulders.

"Thanks, Daddy."

Snap. Snap.

"All right, now Willow, you get in."

"Wait!" Willow shouts. "What about Gigi?"

"Oh, no, baby. Y'all need a family picture." Gina starts backing away slowly.

"Babe..." I wave her over. "Get in here." She was such a huge part of this day and *is* such an integral part of our lives. She belongs in the photos.

"It's fine, Jeff. I don't need to be in the picture."

Evangeline walks over, grabbing Tink by the arm and pulls. "Get in the damn picture, Gina."

"Evangeline!" I warn. "Language."

"Everyone says damn, Daddy." My daughter huffs, completely disregarding my reprimand.

"Yeah, well—"

"I know. I know," Vangie mocks. "I'm not everyone else's daughter."

"THIS IS THE BEST DOUBLE date everrr!" Willow squeals, skipping toward the entrance to the zoo in her poufy yellow Belle dress.

A less enthusiastic pirate growls, behind her. "It's not a date, Willow. Argh! Don't make me cut you with my sword."

"How many years do you think it'll be before they're hiding behind the trees between you and Spencer's houses to make out?" Gina teases, squeezing my hand.

"Stop it." My eyes veer to the side, narrowing. "I don't even wanna think about that right now."

Gina giggles, cuddling into my side. She looks like a sexy little Eskimo all bundled up in her marshmallow jacket. You'd swear by looking at her it was like twenty degrees out rather than the refreshing sixty.

"Willow and Savage, get your little butts back over here before someone steals you," I shout when they start getting a little too far ahead of us.

"You say that like it'd be a bad thing," Tink teases.

"Knowing our luck...they'd bring 'em back."

"Yook, Daddy!" Willow runs over with her candy bag opened wide. "Them nice wadies gave me tandy."

"That's great. Now stay right here while Daddy pays."

"Welcome to Boo at the Zoo. Two adults and two children...

That'll be 36.50."

"Kyle, a man always pays for his date. Where's your money?" I hold out my hand, teasing, and that little punk licks it! "Gross!"

"I'm not on a date and don't got no money. Looks like you're shit outta luck, CEO."

"Kyle!" Gina gasps before losing her temporary lapse into adulthood and folding at the waist in a fit of hysterics. "Oh my God, you are such a savage."

Kyle beams. It's no wonder the kid says the things he does with the reaction he gets, but I don't dare comment on the matter. He isn't mine, and despite his potty mouth, he really is a sweet kid.

"Sorry, ma'am." My cheeks heat as I hand the woman my card to pay for our admission. "He's not mine," I whisper when she passes it back with the receipt and a pen.

The woman laughs, exchanging our tickets for the card receipt. "Y'all have a great time."

"Yet's go see the unicorns!" Willow begs, tilting her head to the side and fluttering those long lashes. She's such a little flirt already.

"Willow, unicorns aren't—"

"Out tonight," Tink interrupts, glaring my way. "How 'bout we go check out the zebras instead?"

"What the heck?" I ask Tink as we navigate our way through the crowd to the zebra enclosure.

"She's three. You gonna tell her Santa isn't real, too, Mr. Grinch?" Gina hisses. "Let her believe in magic, Jeff. It's the best part of being a little girl."

What did I do before Tink? "Don't ever leave me," I say, pulling her in for a kiss while the kids are occupied at the fence arguing over whether the damn zebras are white with black stripes or black with white. "You'll ruin her childhood."

"Mr. Ryan," Gina purrs against my lips. "That sounds like bribery."

"I'm a desperate man, Ms. Bourque."

"Ewwww," Willow and Kyle shout in unison.

"How tome you tan tiss Gigi, and I tan't tiss Tyle?" my little girl asks as Gina and I separate.

"Because," I say, swiping a hand over my lips. "We're in love."

Before any of us realizes what's happening, my daughter turns to the side, planting a kiss right on Kyle's cheek.

"Hey!" he shouts, rubbing it away. "You do that again, I'm gonna punch you in the face."

"You most certainly will not punch her, Kyle," Gina warns.

"I better never see you do that again, Willow Jane." What the heck just happened?

"Well, next time you better cwose you eyes, then, Daddy. Cuz me and Tyle is in yove."

"Ugh, no. No, Willow. I am not in love," Kyle argues, still scrubbing at the spot where she just violated him.

"How about the monkeys?" Gina suggests, grabbing each of the kids by the hand, effectively separating them, one on each side of her body.

Dear God. The zoo animals are tame compared to these two.

The monkeys are right around the corner in a roped-off area, surrounded by a moat to keep them on their little monkey island. There are ropes to climb and swing on, and hammocks for them to rest.

"Yook at that one," Willow says, pointing to one of the larger monkeys. He walks right out to the edge of the island

and sits, facing the crowd.

"I think he likes the attention," Gina observes. "Kinda like two other monkeys I know."

I stand back a little, just watching her with the children. She's a natural. So patient and loving.

"What's him doing?" Willow asks.

"Uhhh," Gina hedges, looking over her shoulder at me for help.

"He's shakin' up his baby juice," Savage answers, all matter of fact. "Those are his tenticles, and they're compartments that hold seeds that are really babies. Then—this is the best part— he can shoot 'em inside a girl tummy to make a baby, with his *penis*."

Squeezing between the small crowd separating us, I force my way to the front. The fucking monkey has a hand between its legs, and he's jiggling his balls. "Close your eyes, Willow... Savage—"

"Oh my God. Him's gonna pull it off! Him's gonna break his baby juice gun," Willow shouts.

Gina is of no help to the mini panic attack I have going on internally. The woman can't get a word out because she's laughing so hard. God love her.

"Time to go!" My announcement is met with grunts and grumbles. "Don't start that. We need to get back before Evangeline and Landon, anyway."

The trek back is miserable, but the kids are asleep before we've even gotten out of the parking lot. "What a freaking night." My eyes wander to the side, meeting Tink's. "Where does he come up with this shit?" I ask, referring to tonight's lesson on monkey reproduction.

"Well," she drawls, blushing. "That one might be a little bit my fault."

Why doesn't that surprise me in the least?

Chapter Thirty-Nine

JEFFREY

Tears build in my eyes as I stand off to the side, watching the stylist add the final touches to her hair and makeup. When she pins the tiara in place, my breath catches in my throat. She's literally the most beautiful bride I've ever seen. Her dress is fit for a queen, made of silk and lace, with tulle underneath to give her the full skirt she's always wanted. After stepping into her silver, strappy pumps and taking a moment to admire herself in the floor-length mirror, she reaches out for my hand. I close my fingers around hers, lifting them as I bend to place a kiss on her knuckles before leading my princess out to the backyard where the ceremony is to take place.

No detail has been spared. White wood chairs line both sides of the pink petal-covered aisle. The trellis is dripping with baby's breath and expertly placed pink roses. All of our family and loved ones are gathered, dressed to the nines, to celebrate this special occasion. It would be so easy to focus on the pain surrounding this day, but I will always associate November twenty-fifth not with what we lost, but with the birth of this beautiful angel standing beside me.

When the music starts up and our eyes lock, my heart skips a beat. This little girl is joy personified. There is nothing in this world I wouldn't do for her.

"You ready?" I ask, squeezing her hand. She nods, and as I walk her down the aisle preparing to give her away, I become overwrought with emotion. That is until I see the sheer horror on the face of her groom. *That little shit.*

When we're mere feet away and I finally catch his attention. I rub the thumb and forefinger of my free hand together, signing a reminder of the fifty bucks I had to promise this kid to marry my daughter. That's okay. In another fifteen to twenty years, he'll be begging for her hand, and I'll get my revenge.

I place her hand into his and lean in close. "To get the money, you have to pretend to want to marry her, Kyle," I warn. Instantly his face perks up.

Throughout the ceremony he holds a smile so big, I think his face may split in two. He really wants that money.

"And now," my brother Victor, who is acting as officiant, says as he adjusts his tie, trying not to laugh. "You may kiss the bride."

Willow's eyes flutter closed as she leans in, puckering her little lips. Savage arches his back trying to get away. Then, he shoves a finger down his throat with an exaggerated gag, and the crowd erupts into a chorus of giggles.

"I'm waiting, Tyle..." she says, still holding her practiced position.

A panic washes over me. I didn't come this far to have her dream wedding ruined. Grabbing a hundred-dollar bill from my wallet, I rush to the altar, holding it out in front of his face. I point to my cheek and pucker my lips. That little shit nods and holds his hand out, palm up. Evidently a kiss requires prepayment. After tucking the bill into his palm, I rush back to my seat beside the woman I love. The woman who spent weeks preparing this special day for my baby girl.

Kyle shoves the money into his pocket then leans in, planting a quick peck to the side of her face before rubbing his lips on the sleeve of his tux jacket. "Bleh!"

The smile on Willow's face is everything. For a moment I catch myself wishing that Jessica could be here to see how happy our baby girl is. I know she'd be proud. I don't always get it right, but this time...this time I know that I did.

"She sees," Tink says, reading my expression perfectly. I don't know how she knows me so well, at times even better than I know myself.

She rests her hand on my thigh, and I lay mine on top of hers, squeezing affectionately when Victor announces, "I now pronounce you husband and wife."

A three-tier wedding cake is brought out on a linen-covered table by Lake and Landon with four sparklers lit on the top. Willow blushes a deep crimson when everyone joins in singing the happy birthday song.

Gina kisses my cheek then rushes over to the table to cut the cake. The first plate goes to the birthday girl. The second to her new *husband*. When Kyle lifts a hunk of cake to his mouth, Willow shouts, "Stop!"

"What're you screaming about now?"

"You have to feed me, Tyle, and I have to feed you. Don't you know anyting?"

Kyle's face screws up in confusion. "CEO! Deal with your daughter. I'm hungry."

"Boy! I just paid your ass a hundred dollars to marry Willow.

You can damn sure feed her a bite of cake."

"Ooooh, Daddy, you saided a sentence hancer." Willow's eyes grow big and round with shock, and Kyle snickers beside her.

"Sorry, your husband's language is rubbing off on me," I tease.

After cake, Cooper starts up the music he's prepared, and Kyle fulfills his duty, giving Willow the obligatory first dance as man and wife.

"Tale as Old as Time," from the *Beauty and the Beast* soundtrack—Willow's current obsession—starts up, and the miniature bride and groom walk out to the center of the patio. They join hands, keeping a wide birth between them. While they spin around the makeshift dancefloor, Gina and Spencer snap photos from every angle, instructing them when to smile, where to look, when to spin.

I can't stop smiling at the two women fawning all over my little girl. She may no longer have a mother living on earth, but I'm so thankful for these two who've stepped in to fill that void in her life. Moving here, while I'll admit was a bit crazy and spontaneous, turned out to be the best thing for us all.

"Tank you, Daddy," Willow squeals, running with her arms spread wide when their dance has ended. "This was the bestest birthday ever!"

"You're welcome, princess. I'm so happy you loved it. But, you need to go thank your Gigi and Spence. They did all the work. Daddy just wrote the checks." I explain as my eyes lock with Tink's across the room. She nibbles on her lower lip, giving me a sexy little wink.

"What's a sheck?" Willow asks, cupping my cheeks and turning my face back to hers.

"Money, Willow. Checks are money."

"Well, den..." Her little lips plant a kiss right in the center of my forehead. "Tank you for your moneys."

Laughing, I set her back down on the floor. "My pleasure. Now go thank the real MVPs." I motion to Spence and Gina, finding she's still staring my way.

"What's a MPP?"

"Just go say thank you, Willow!" This girl can be so exasperating at times.

Once the party begins to wind down, the big kids take the littles inside to watch a movie, and the adults break out the karaoke machine. I wait until everyone's had a few rounds of drinks and butchered a song or two before breaking out the guitar and giving Tink a little gift of her own.

"You play guitar?" she asks, wide-eyed and grinning ear to ear as I strum the beginning chords to "In Case You Didn't Know," by Brett Young.

Every word that I sing is a message to this beautiful woman staring back at me, who's managed to become the beat of my heart in such a short amount of time. It's my every feeling professed in front of our friends and family. My heart laid bare.

Before I've even set the guitar down, she's in my arms. Her hands grip my hair, and Tink pulls my mouth to hers, whispering, "I'm crazy 'bout you too, Jeff Ryan." Then, our lips connect and fireworks explode around us.

Or, you know, it could just be the sound of our idiotic friends clapping and howling.

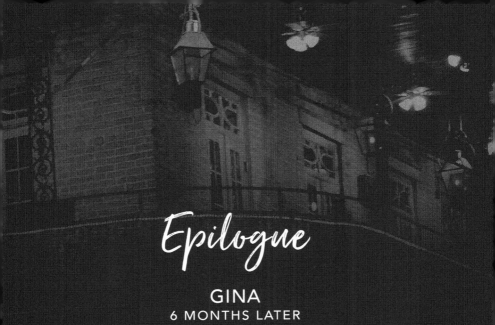

Epilogue

GINA
6 MONTHS LATER

"J eff?" I call out into the seemingly empty house after letting myself in with my key. Where the hell is he? He made it seem so urgent when he called and asked me to come over.

"Out here!" he shouts through the doors leading out to the back patio. I set my purse and keys on the table near the front door and follow the sound of little girl giggles out back.

"Do you wike him?" Willow asks, lifting a fluffy white puppy into her arms.

"I love him," I say, bending to kiss the top of her head and pet the little ball of fluff. "You finally got them a puppy?" I can feel the look of confusion on my own face. Jeffrey is not an animal person. He swore he'd never allow one.

"Us," Evangeline says, finally lifting her eyes from the cellphone that never seems to leave her hand these days. I'd bet money that she's talking to my godson.

"I said, y'all, goober. I meant you too."

"No, her means Charlie is for me and Vangie and you," Willow clarifies.

"Awwww, are you going to share your puppy with me?" My eyes get a little misty. I've always wanted a dog, but my apartment doesn't allow pets. "That's so sweet of you." I guess they figure since I'm always over here anyway, we'll be spending a lot of time together.

"You have to move in, Gina," Evangeline says from where she's still perched on her chair near the wrought iron table with her feet curled beneath her legs. "Dad said it's the only way we can keep him."

What the hell is going on? I'm starting to feel a little ambushed and a hell of a lot of confused.

"What my daughter is so eloquently trying to say," Jeffrey says walking over from where he's been busily preparing our dinner at the pit. "Is we would love it. All three—"

"Four," Willow interrupts, pointing to the puppy.

Jeff apologizes. "All *four* of us would love nothing more than for you to move in with us."

My entire body starts to shake, and I can't seem to swallow. "You're asking me to l—live here? In this house? Like get rid of my place and stay here permanently with you?"

"Gina," Jeff, coos, lifting my face to meet his. "I love you."

My head starts to shake of its own accord, and warm, wet tears stream down my face. "I love you too, CEO. Goddamn it. I didn't want to."

"I know," he says, laughing. "I'm just so damn charming."

"I love them too," I add, looking to the two little girls who've managed to steal my heart. "I love you both so much."

"I wuv you too, Gigi." My heart swells, but it's when Evangeline sets her phone on the table and walks over, throwing her arms around my neck, that I completely fucking lose it. "I love you, Gina. Everything is so much better with you here. Please say yes."

"Are you sure?" I ask Jeffrey, who's looking at me like he wants to devour me.

His answer is to drop down on his knee. *Oh, God. Oh, God. Oh. My. God.*

"If there's one thing life has taught me, it's not to take a single day for granted. Gina, you make me happier than I've been in years. I didn't think I was capable of loving again so deeply. You burst into our lives like a bomb, when our world needed nothing more than to be shaken up."

I can't help but to laugh at his description.

"Tink, you breathe life into this family. If you'll have me—if you'll have us—we want to make you ours forever. Gina Bourque, I'm on my knees, offering you everything you've ever wanted. Two," he points to the girls, "and a half," he gestures to himself with a shrug, "kids and a white fluffy dog."

My God, I can't believe he remembered that conversation from all those months back.

"It's not the Garden District, but believe me when I say this house was bought with you in mind. It has all of the same charm, with your friends and family nearby."

"I don't know what to say," I stammer.

"I will devote my life to giving you everything you deserve. More love than you ever thought possible. Gina, baby, will you marry me?"

"Put him outta his misewy aweady, Gigi."

Through a torrent of tears, I snort out a laugh, my emotions all over the place. "Yes," I whisper, nodding my head. I cup my right hand to the side of his face, smoothing away his tears with my thumb, as he slides a beautiful antique diamond engagement ring onto my finger.

"Yes," I repeat, a little louder. Then I throw myself into his arms, knocking him off balance, and we go tumbling into the yard. Willow decides she wants in on the pile-up, jumping right on top. Then, of course, Charlie follows suit, shaking his fluffy little butt all up in our faces.

"Get in here, Vange," Jeff urges. "First official family hug."

As little girls, we have big dreams. Our perfect family. The perfect life. All too often things don't go according to plan. But if you're lucky, like me, you just might end up with something so much better, so much *bigger* than anything you ever imagined.

As I lay here in the arms of the people I love, it no longer matters how we got here. All that matters is that we've found a home in each other, and wherever we go, whatever we do...we do it together.

Extended Epilogue

SAVAGE
AGE 16
(12 YEARS LATER)

"We'd like to ask that everyone please clear the dance floor as we welcome our bride and groom, Landon and Evangeline Tate, for their first dance as husband and wife!"

The lights in the reception hall dim, and everyone moves to make a circle around the newlyweds. Gigi and Mom—and pretty much every woman in attendance and even some of the men—are dabbing at tears in their eyes, and I'm just ready to get this thing over with so I can get out of this damn tux. It's not like it's any surprise these two tied the knot. They've been together forever. People are so strange.

"Don't they look amazing?" Willow whispers, all dreamy-like, as she suddenly appears at my side. "We're practically related now. Isn't that weird?"

"We're not related," I snap, trying not to stare at her boobs in the tight pink bridesmaid dress that's been giving me heart palpitations since I watched her step out of that limo two hours ago. She looks different—she looks *hot*. Her blonde hair is all curly and styled, and she's wearing makeup.

"Grouchy much?" she asks, nudging me with her elbow. "What's wrong, Kyle?"

"Nothing. I'm just ready to take this bowtie off."

Her hands move to straighten it, and my heart starts beating a little faster. She smells like perfume. Willow never wears perfume. I'm starting to feel a little dizzy. Her being this close, Smelling so fucking good and looking like she belongs in a magazine. "There." She pats her hands on my chest a few times and turns back to watch the couple. "Should be looser now. Is it better?"

"Yeah, thanks."

Willow beams, then her eyes start to glisten as she watches our siblings make out on the dance floor, swaying to the tune of "I Love the Way You Love Me" by John Michael Montgomery.

"Oh, God. Not you too?"

"What?" she says, sniffling.

"Don't you fucking cry, Lo." She knows I can't stand it when she acts like a wuss. Really, I just hate to see her cry. I can't handle that shit, and she knows it. No matter how much she gets on my nerves, I feel like I have to find a way to fix it. It's probably her damn dad's fault for always making me feel responsible for her.

"Don't tell me what to do, asshole. I'll cry if I wanna."

Before I can respond, everyone's clapping and cheering, and the D.J. comes back over the mic, inviting the wedding party to the floor.

"Guess that's us," I say linking my arm through hers. "Come on crybaby."

We reach the middle of the floor just as the song begins. "You Look Wonderful Tonight" by Eric Clapton drifts from the speakers. My best friend's arms curl around my neck as I wrap mine around her tiny waist, and we sway side to side to the beat of the music. I sing the chorus into her ear, and it sort of freaks me out how much I actually mean what I'm saying. As the song goes on, I start to panic, because I don't want it to end. Don't want Willow's boobs to leave my chest. And God, I want to keep feeling the heat of her breath on my neck. It's making me dizzy in the best possible way.

"Lo?" I rasp, barely recognizing my own voice. Why do I sound nervous? I don't get nervous, especially not with Willow.

"Yeah?"

"You really do look beautiful."

Even in the dim lighting I can see her cheeks turning pink. "Thanks, Savage."

"I think I wanna kiss you," I blurt out, and immediately I wish I could take the words back, because this is my fucking best friend. What am I even thinking? Her dad will kill me.

Willow's body tenses in my arms, and she pulls back a little, looking me right in the eyes. "You do?"

Fuck it. I might as well finish what I've just started. "Yeah. I think I do."

"Our parents are watching," she whispers into my ear, her voice shaking.

"Come walk with me by the lake? When we finish pictures and all that bullshit."

Her arms tighten to the point that she's nearly choking me. "Okay." She nods. "But I've never kissed anyone before, Kyle. I—I might not be good at it."

Something tells me she'll be better than good. "It's not

hard, Lo. I'll show you."

She nods just as the song finishes, and we're whisked apart and drug over to the cake table. The photos are seemingly endless. And the time is multiplied because I know what awaits when we finish.

WHEN OUR PARENTS AND SIBLINGS are once again distracted, I grab Willow's hand and motion for the back exit. Neither of us breathes a word until the door slams shut behind us.

"You cold?" I ask, feeling her hand start to tremble in mine.

She nods, curling into my side as we navigate the rocky path leading down to the wrought iron bench that sits near the lake.

Slipping out of my jacket, I place it over her shoulders. "Here."

Willow dips her face down into the collar and inhales. "Mmm," she moans. "Smells like you." Hah. My mom would argue that's not a good thing.

"Come closer, Lo," I rasp when she sits almost a foot away from me on the bench.

Hesitantly she scoots in. "Kyle?"

"Yeah?"

"Is this...Is this gonna change things with us?" How have I never noticed how beautiful this girl is?

I think for a moment before answering, because this is Willow, not just some chick from school. "Probably."

Nodding, she leans in closer. "I'm ready."

With one arm wrapped around her back and the hand of the other cupping the side of her face, I lean in, pressing my lips to hers. I don't use my tongue until she's loosened up a little. Until her hands are gripping my shirt and she's climbing into my lap. Then I dive in, swirling my tongue around with hers.

"Kyle," she murmurs into my mouth as her fingers knot in my hair.

"Hmm?"

"Are you still gonna kiss Riley?" she asks, her eyes welling up again.

"No," I answer, nipping at her lips, her chin, her neck. "Just you, Lo."

"Good. Then, I won't kiss anyone else either."

"Damn right you won't," I growl before sucking her bottom lip into my mouth. We're all tongues and teeth and panting breaths.

"There you two a—"

Oh, shit. It's the CEO.

Willow hops out of my lap like her ass is on fire, both of us wiping our wet lips on the backs of our hands.

"Dammit," her father huffs, shaking his head in disappointment. "Here we go again."

Acknowledgements

Aaaaand book four is a wrap! Wow. This is always the scariest part for me. So many people are vital to this process and I'm terrified to forget one. But here goes...

First and foremost, thank you to my husband, Adam. And to my children; Xavier, Bari, Kari, Parker, Amelia, and Kellan (aka Savage). You sacrifice so much for this dream of mine and I love and appreciate you more than you know.

My tripod. Kate and Lo, I'm a writer with no words. There aren't words for what the two of you mean to me. You're here for me always. Picking up my slack. Encouraging me when I can't go anymore. You are the true definition of best friends and I love you both more than Pepsi and Tootsie Rolls.

Lo, you get a special shout-out for this badass title. Thank you for thinking of me the moment you heard it and knowing me enough to realize how perfect it was.

Juliana. This cover!!! Thank you for everything you do for me. From covers, to formatting, to talking me off the ledge. For making me giggle and encouraging me. For your amazing design skills, because I never know what I want. LOL You go above and beyond the call of duty and I'm so grateful to call you my friend.

My new editor, Kiezha. Making this change was not easy for me. To be honest, I was terrified. Thank you for being understanding and patient with me. You did an amazing job making my words beautiful and I'm so excited to work with you again!

Nicole and Dani, the two best alpha/beta readers there are. You put up with more of my insecurities than anyone else. I'm needy and dramatic and I love you both for your constant support and encouragement. You helped make this book what it is.

Shanora, my Felicia...You are my rock. Thank you for always being there for me when I need an ear and being one of the best damn friends a girl could ask for. I love you.

To the best reader group there is. Thank you, Hunnies! Your enthusiasm and support keeps me going.

David Wagner, you are a fantastic photographer and a joy to work with. Thank you for everything!

To my Minxes and DND author friends. THANK YOU! Your wealth of knowledge and support is endless. I'm blessed to have you all on my side.

To the girls of Give Me Books, you rock my world. Book FOUR, ladies! You are always so professional and such a joy to work with. Thank you so much for all that you do to support me.

Thank you to all of the bloggers and readers who pick up my books and take a chance on me over and over again. I couldn't do this without you.

About the Author

Heather M. Orgeron is a Cajun girl with a big heart and a passion for romance. She married her high school sweetheart two months after graduation and her life has been a fairytale ever since. She's the queen of her castle, reigning over five sons and one bossy little princess who has made it her mission in life to steal her Momma's throne. When she's not writing, you will find her hidden beneath mounds of laundry and piles of dirty dishes or locked in her tower (aka the bathroom) soaking in the tub with a good book. She's always been an avid reader and has recently discovered a love for cultivating romantic stories of her own.

If you would like to connect with
Heather M. Orgeron, you can find her here:

Facebook: facebook.com/AuthorHeatherMOrgeron
Reader Group: facebook.com/groups/1738663433047683/
Twitter: twitter.com/hmorgeronauthor
Instagram: instagram.com/heather_m_orgeron_author

Made in the USA
Columbia, SC
13 September 2021